"I don't want to frighten you away again."

Taylor's hand gently squeezed Jillian's shoulder as he asked, "Can we try being friends?"

Friends! When a casual touch from him could reduce her insides to jelly? But anything was better than not being with him. "Yes, of course," she said huskily.

"Then will you have dinner with us tonight? I promise I won't do anything you don't want yourself," he pressed persuasively.

The whole problem was what she did want. But she could not deny herself the pleasure of his company, no matter how great the risk of being hurt. "All right," she agreed quickly.

There were only eight days left of the charter. Eight days to make the most of Taylor's offer of friendship and, if at all possible, to win his heart....

EMMA DARCY nearly became an actress until her fiancé declared he preferred to attend the theatre *with* her. She became a wife and mother. Later she took up oil painting—unsuccessfully, she remarks. Then, she tried architecture, designing the family home in New South Wales. Next came romance writing—"the hardest and most challenging of all the activities," she confesses.

Books by Emma Darcy

EMMA DARCY

the one that got away

Harlequin Books

**TORONTO • NEW YORK • LONDON
AMSTERDAM • PARIS • SYDNEY • HAMBURG
STOCKHOLM • ATHENS • TOKYO • MILAN**

For Bob—
in gratitude for all his help—
and with every wish that The Patriots might
win this year!

Harlequin Presents first edition December 1987
ISBN 0-373-11033-2

Original hardcover edition published in 1987
by Mills & Boon Limited

CHAPTER ONE

THE Boeing 727 flew a long, lazy circle inside the ring of mountains surrounding Cairns before it swung out to sea and lined up with the runway. Jillian viewed it with apprehension. The people she had to meet were not going to like what she had to tell them. They were not going to like it at all. She locked the car and rubbed a slightly sweaty palm down her skirt. At least she had made it to the airport in time for their arrival, and with a few minutes to spare in which to compose herself.

Her stomach was a cramped knot as she entered the reception lounge of the terminal. She caught a glimpse of her reflection in the glass doors as they swung shut again. It was some small consolation to know that her appearance was attractive enough to make a good first impression.

Her yellow sundress with the white shell-print was a typical tourist style, bright and cool and sexy. The white and yellow strappy sandals had a high enough heel to emphasise the shapeliness of her long, tanned legs. In keeping with the sophisticated image of her boutique, she had piled her blonde hair into a loose chignon on top of her crown and made the most of her large blue eyes with subtle make-up. A pretty concoction of shells dangled from her ears. Unfortunately, the customers she was about to meet were going to be harder to impress than the customers who dropped into her boutique.

They had come for one purpose, the one purpose which brought anglers from all around the world to the Great Barrier Reef for three months of the year. They wanted to try their hand at catching the giant black marlin, and they wanted that catch so much they had chartered the lead boat of the fishing fleet and the lead skipper. They were certainly not going to like what she had to tell them.

The jet engines roared into reverse as the plane touched down on the runway. Only a few minutes left now. Jillian told herself to keep cool, calm and collected as she watched the plane taxi up to the passenger tunnel. She must not get flustered. So much depended upon her projecting absolute confidence. Even the smallest sign of uneasiness might be sufficient to cut the only thread of hope she had left. And then ... disaster!

People started streaming down the walkway. Jillian took a deep breath and forced an easy, relaxed smile. The American party would undoubtedly have flown first-class, which meant they would be amongst the first to enter the terminal. Four men with American accents. They should be easy to spot.

Even in her highly nervous state, and all too aware of the importance of her mission, Jillian could not help staring at the first man who came through the doors. He looked to be about thirty years old and he was all man, all six feet of him. She had never seen such a superb physique on anyone, despite all the sportsmen who streamed through Cairns. His jeans and T-shirt clung to a stunning arrangement of masculine muscle and his face was equally striking.

Strong and sort of Aztec-looking, Jillian mused, with
a mouthful of gleaming white teeth and hair that was
thick and black and shiny. The man exuded health
and energy as if he was a dynamo in temporary
harness.

He caught her stare and winked at her. A flush of
embarrassment and self-anger heightened the natural
colour in her cheeks. Her father was facing a crippling
financial loss and here she was being distracted by a
man! She refocused her mind on the all-important
job, yet she was conscious of the man taking a long,
leisurely appraisal of her. It plunged her emotions
into more confusion. She wanted to look back at him
but she couldn't. Her father was counting on her. She
had no time for any men except the ones she had to
meet.

An American accent drew her attention. A party of
three men were conversing among themselves as they
entered the lounge. The lead man looked to be the
typical managerial type and was speaking in a tone of
authority. He was fortyish, lean, conscious of his
dignity in light grey slacks, a pink and white striped
shirt and grey tie. Surely her mark, Jillian decided.
She fixed a bright smile on her face, tried to steady
her galloping pulse, hoped that her voice would
operate on command, and made her approach.

'Mr Taylor Marshall?'

Pale blue eyes swept her with open appreciation.
There was something in those eyes, a cynical
measuring that made Jillian bristle with antagonism.
She felt reduced to a lump of female meat, quite
delectable but of no account in the real world except
as a pleasurable diversion.

'No, ma'am. I'm Earl Schultz.' He flashed a nicotine-stained grin. 'But I am Taylor Marshall's agent and manager. Taylor . . .'

Jillian turned to find the handsome face she had admired smiling with amusement. It was him! Her large blue eyes could not help sparkling with pleasant surprise. 'Mr Marshall . . .'

'At your service, ma'am.' His voice was a deep, honeyed drawl which somehow suggested all the bedroom knowledge in the world. 'Any time,' he added suggestively.

He had it all, Jillian mused. Sex appeal plus. And he knew it! She sent an urgent command to her suddenly acrobatic heart. Calm, cool and collected, she reminded herself, and thrust out a hand which was instantly enclosed in a warm grasp. 'I'm Jillian Howard, Jack Howard's daughter. Welcome to Australia, North Queensland, Cairns, and the Great Barrier Reef, Mr Marshall. And Mr Schultz,' she included belatedly.

'I'm astonished you didn't recognise Taylor, Miss Howard,' Earl Schultz remarked with a hint of chagrin. 'Haven't you seen *Forbidden Fruit*?'

What in God's name was *Forbidden Fruit*? The last thing she wanted to do was to get these people off-side. Her mind whirled with feverish necessity. Inspiration struck. 'Er . . . is that a movie?'

'Biggest hit on the screen in the States,' Earl Shultz declared with a hint of exasperation at her ignorance. 'With Taylor in the leading role,' he added to punch home the point.

A movie star! Oh God! Why hadn't her father warned her? Because he had too much else to worry about, that's why. Desperate to recover lost ground,

Jillian switched on an appeasing smile. 'I'm sorry, Mr Marshall. I don't go to many movies.'

His smile did nothing to ease the agitated flutter of her heart. 'Wouldn't bother going to see it myself, Miss Howard. I'm more of a football player than an actor.'

A football player! Jillian's mind reeled again. Was there something else she was supposed to know?

'Taylor happens to be the leading quarterback in the football league, Miss Howard.' Earl Schultz enlightened her, almost grating his teeth. 'Voted the most valuable player of the year.'

Oh God! I've really bumbled, Jillian thought with a sinking heart. What do they expect me to do? Bow and scrape? No. Apology wasn't going to get her anywhere in this situation. She had to get these people firmly placed on her home ground. Her smile moved up another brightness notch. 'Well, it's plain to see you've arrived Down Under, Mr Marshall. I'm totally ignorant of American football. I don't even know what a quarterback is.'

'Then it will be my pleasure to teach you, Miss Howard,' he replied smoothly.

His bedroom-brown eyes were taking a detailed inventory of her assets, and she only just managed not to squirm with pleasure under their melting survey. He was dynamite all right. Pull yourself together, Jillian, she commanded. It was imperative that she concentrate on the important business in hand. When was the best time to tell them? Not yet, she decided.

'My father sent me to meet you. I understand there are four in your party?'

Earl Schultz snapped his fingers at the other two

men who had moved aside to watch for the appearance of their luggage on the conveyor belt. 'Jerry ... Gordon ... come and meet our skipper's daughter.'

Jillian tore her eyes away from Taylor Marshall and hid her unease at the mention of 'skipper'. Reason told her to play up to their desire for the big catch before hitting them with the news about her father. Every instinct clamoured to delay the moment of reckoning.

The two men who answered the summons were a sharp contrast; one obviously an outdoors man, strong and wiry, his face weather-lined even though he was only in his twenties; the other was closer to Earl Schultz's age, short, sharp-looking and pallid. The latter was introduced first.

'Jerry Somers is our cameraman. Jerry, meet Miss Jillian Howard.'

She smiled and offered her hand even as she wondered why they had gone to the expense of bringing a cameraman from America. The normal procedure was to hire a local photographer if a charter wanted a video-record of his catch.

Jerry Somers enlightened her. 'Hope to get some fantastic shots, Miss Howard. Earl here wants a video of Taylor catching a world record marlin. A film of that could be great publicity for him.'

Jillian's heart sank. They expected so much! Even with her father they would have been hard pressed to ...

'That's what we've come for,' Earl crowed. 'Nothing like a world record to make a big splash! Taylor's career in films is just taking off and I aim to promote him to the top. We're going to get some great publicity out of this, and to ensure that everything goes right, we've hired the best boat, the best skipper, and brought the best deck-hand in Florida with us. Don't want any incompetents on board with us, do we, Gordon? Gordon Duffy, Miss Howard.'

Despite the fact that her heart was now down to her sandals, Jillian could not let that statement go unchallenged. 'Cairns is the Mecca of big-game fishing, Mr Schultz. Any deckie who gets a job on one of the boats in the fishing fleet has to be the best in the world. I hope your Mr Duffy is up to it.'

The deckie grinned. 'I've been everywhere, Miss Howard. Florida, Mexico, Peru . . .'

'What's the biggest fish you've pulled in, Mr Duffy?'

'Just over eight hundred pounds.'

'A baby compared to the giant black marlin we catch here, Mr Duffy.'

'Hear that, Taylor?' Earl broke in excitedly. 'How many has your father hooked up this season, Miss Howard? Big ones!'

She grabbed the opportunity to whet their appetite for the chase. 'Twelve over a thousand pounds, Mr Schultz. One fourteen-hundred pounder. Dad reckoned he had one world record on the line but the angler wasn't strong enough to hold it.'

'No worries there, eh, Taylor?'

'I hope not,' came the non-committal answer.

The luggage started its first revolution and everyone moved towards the belt, all except Taylor Marshall. Jillian had been aware of his close observation of her throughout the short conversation with his cohorts and now he turned the full force of his smile on her.

'I daresay you've landed quite a few ... fish yourself, Miss Howard,' he said with a suggestive lilt.

None more important than what she had to land now, Jillian thought, and that meant using every advantage at her disposal. If Taylor Marshall found her attractive enough to bother with suggestive statements, then maybe he could be sweet-talked into keeping on the charter. She batted her long eyelashes. 'Not as big as you, I'm sure, Mr Marshall.'

He chuckled, a deep, attractive rumble which sent tingles down Jillian's spine.

'Well, I don't know much about Down Under, Miss Howard, but what little I've seen I like very much. Perhaps you can teach me a few things.'

'I'd be delighted to, Mr Marshall. What would you like to know?'

'Whether all the girls in Australia are as pretty as you?'

She laughed, more out of embarrassment than amusement. Did he really think her pretty or was he simply amusing himself with her? 'I thought you'd come to view the beauty of the Great Barrier Reef, Mr Marshall. I assure you it's a unique experience. I can't imagine that pretty girls are at all unique for you, but what we have to offer here cannot be found anywhere else in the world.'

His eyes twinkled roguishly. 'I'm beginning to believe it.'

'Where to now, Miss Howard?' Earl Schultz cut in.

The luggage had been loaded on to a trolley. She cast a smile around the whole party. 'If you'll just follow me I'll drive you into the city to meet my father, and then to the Pacific International Hotel where you're booked in for the night.'

'Your father not fishing today?' Taylor Marshall asked as they strolled out to the car park.

'Uh ... no. He's ... er ... resting up,' she prevaricated, not wanting to drop the bombshell before she had to. Correct timing was of the essence. If she could just put in a bit more groundwork ...

'Well, that does surprise me,' Earl Schultz commented critically. 'I would've thought the lead boat had to be out every day of the season if it's to keep its record.'

'Dad's last charter was happy to call it a day this morning.' With a refund of twelve hundred dollars, Jillian added grimly to herself. If Taylor Marshall pulled out of his charter, her father was going to face a loss of seventeen thousand dollars. If the rest of the season had to be cancelled, it would be financial disaster. Her father would almost certainly lose his boat.

They reached her car and she quickly unlocked it. After some determined re-arrangement, the luggage was finally fitted into the boot. Taylor Marshall commandeered the front passenger seat and the other three men squashed into the back. As Jillian settled herself behind the wheel he threw her a look of intimate interest. 'We sure appreciate this VIP service, Miss Howard.'

'It's always a pleasure to welcome visitors, Mr Marshall,' she smiled at him, all flags flying. In his particular case it was true. She wished the circumstances were different.

'Do you always meet your father's charters?'

'Quite often,' she half-lied, avoiding the trap of letting him know that this trip was pure emergency stations. Her adrenalin was working overtime.

'And the rest of the time?'

'I run a dress boutique.'

'Taylor, we're here for the fishing,' Earl Schultz remarked drily from the back seat. 'A world record, remember?'

'Now how could I forget that, Earl?' came the slightly mocking retort. He raised a sardonic eyebrow at Jillian. 'Anyone beaten the old record this season, Miss Howard?'

She sliced him a brilliant smile. 'No, it's out there waiting for you, Mr Marshall.' If old George has agreed to skipper, if you accept the change, if, if, if. She injected a bright optimism into her voice and spoke of the various catches that had been made, embroidering the stories with lyrical descriptions of the strength and beauty of the black marlin.

When she finally brought the car to a halt outside the hospital, the moment of truth could not be put off any longer. Jillian assured herself that no one could have done a better sales job. She desperately hoped that the bottom line which now had to be delivered, would not prove too unpalatable. She had the impression that Taylor Marshall could be persuaded, but Earl Schultz would be very hard to satisfy.

'Is this the hotel?' Taylor asked, a note of surprise in the honeyed drawl.

Since the multi-storeyed building stretched the length of the block it would have been the largest hotel in Australia. Jillian wished it was. She took a deep breath and plunged into the truth. 'No. This is the Cairns Base Hospital. It services all of Cape York. The whole of far North Queensland, actually.'

He looked puzzled. 'So what are we doing here?'

She gave him a look of wide-eyed innocence. 'I'm taking you to see Dad.'

'What's he doing in a hospital?' Earl Schultz asked in a tone of surprise, then, more curtly, 'What's wrong with him?'

Straight to the point. Jillian gritted her teeth into a semblance of a smile. 'He's a bit indisposed. A slight ... er ... accident.'

Taylor Marshall frowned. 'Nothing serious that will put him out of action?'

'For a little while,' Jillian confessed, then added quickly, 'but he's ...'

Earl Schultz cut her off. 'How long?'

Her stomach did a dive. No more evasion now. 'He's slipped a disc, Mr Schultz. It'll probably be three months before ...'

'Three months!' Anger clipped his voice.

Jillian rushed to appease. 'No cause for you to be concerned, Mr Schultz. Dad has arranged to get one of the greatest skippers the North Coast has ever had. If you'll come with me now he'll tell you all about it. Everything is under control. And to your best advantage.'

She hoped. Old George had sworn that nothing would ever drag him out of retirement. She had found him in the Marlin Bar at the Great Northern Hotel, sharing tales of bygone catches with a group of old-timers and fascinated tourists. Golden-tongued with whisky as usual. She had hauled him out and taken

him to her father. The news of her father's accident
had sobered him a little but whether he would agree to
the proposition was still a big question mark.

She hopped out of the car, all bounce and
confidence, denying the queasy pit inside her. Taylor
Marshall and Earl Schultz alighted more slowly,
casting doubtful glances at each other. The cameraman and deckie stayed in the car, apparently
instructed to await developments.

As the two men joined her she saw old George
emerging from the hospital. She waved to attract his
attention. He caught sight of her and a huge grin
spread across his face. Relief surged through her.
Surely he had accepted? It would be all right. He
waited for her to cross the road.

'Talked to your father,' he informed her cheerily.
'Properly laid up, isn't he? But you'll be right, Jilly.'

'Thanks, George,' she said on a deep breath of
gratitude.

He patted her shoulder and moved off before she
thought to introduce him to Taylor Marshall and Earl
Schultz.

'What an old derelict!' the latter commented
contemptuously. 'I could smell the whisky on his
breath from here. Must drink like a fish.'

Her relief dried up. She was so used to seeing old
George in his baggy shorts and crumpled shirts that
she took his careless appearance for granted. The tatty
grey beard and shaggy hair did little to recommend
him as a candidate for sartorial splendour either. And
he had been drinking. He always went on a bender
when he visited Cairns. But she had known him all
her life and the crusty old bachelor had been like a

second father to her. She would have instinctively
defended him anyway, but it was paramount at this
moment to mitigate the poor impression old George
had made on the Americans.

'He ... er ... does have the occasional nip, but
never when he's working,' she said with pointed
emphasis on the 'never'.

'Working!' Taylor Marshall scoffed with a half-
laugh. 'Would anyone give him a job?'

Tact and diplomacy were short-circuited by a
sharp wave of defensive anger. 'Are all your judg-
ments as superficial and instantaneous as that one,
Mr Marshall?'

His eyebrows shot up. The sexy indulgence he had
been beaming at her was suddenly replaced by a sharp
re-calculation. 'I thought I'd seen enough, but I
stand corrected, Miss Howard,' he said softly. 'I
don't usually make a judgment until all the evidence
is in.'

His assurance should have soothed her misgivings
but Jillian found herself prickling under his keen
watchfulness. Taylor Marshall was no fool, and she
had just revealed that the doll he had thought he was
playing with had a bit more mettle under her light
façade. She quickly recomposed her expression to
persuasive charm and suggested they proceed to her
father's room.

If anything, he was in even worse pain than this
morning, Jillian concluded as she observed the
strained pallor of his face. Jack Howard held out his
hand to the two men and tried to inject a welcoming
heartiness into his greeting but Jillian sensed his deep
anxiety. He was not old. Only forty-eight. Yet his

rumpled grey hair and the grey tension in his weather-beaten face made him look sixty.

'Sorry to see you like this,' Taylor Marshall murmured sympathetically.

A half-smile twisted her father's mouth. 'So am I.'

'Why didn't you telex us immediately that you weren't well?' Earl Schultz demanded critically. 'We could have cancelled the whole trip.'

'No point to it. It only happened this morning. You were already half-way here. But I have organised another skipper for you.'

'Who is he? What's his record?'

No sympathy from Earl Schultz, Jillian thought angrily, then chided herself for being unreasonable. He had come a long way to be met by disappointing news. Her father turned his gaze to her, and suddenly Jillian's blood ran cold. More than cold. He couldn't mean . . .

'It's a her. And I've taught her everything I know. She's good. You won't be disappointed.'

Jillian felt faint. Old George had refused the job. But she couldn't do it. She couldn't! Sheer panic curdled her stomach. Her father's eyes clung to hers, desperation peering out of their pain-ridden depths. She had to do it. And somehow she had to make them accept her. Everything depended on it. She pulled herself together and met the dumbstruck looks of the two Americans with a bravado she never knew she had.

'That's right. I'm as good a skipper as Dad any day,' she declared, and prayed that God would not strike her dead for such a terrible lie.

'You!' Earl Schultz was scornfully incredulous.

'You couldn't even have a skipper's ticket!'

'I most certainly have,' Jillian retorted emphatically.

'Since when?' Taylor Marshall asked shrewdly.

'Um...' A quick mental calculation. 'Uh ... fourteen.'

'Since you were fourteen? I don't believe it!' Earl Schultz snarled.

No one would, Jillian quickly realised, and there was no way she could stop them checking such a fact. 'I've only had a skipper's ticket for fourteen days,' she confessed blithely, 'but that doesn't mean ...'

Her father chimed in. 'Jilly's been handling a boat since ...'

Earl Schultz didn't let him finish. He threw up his hands in disgust. 'Forget it! I've just flown half way around the world. I'm very tired and I'm sick of this nonsense. We've put out well in excess of fifty thousand dollars for this trip, the fishing charter, the accommodation on the mother-ship, and our fares. But the contract stated you had to be the skipper. You, Jack Howard. And that's busted wide open. I've had enough! If you can't perform, I don't want anyone else. Certainly not her!'

His pointed finger shook at Jillian's father. 'And I'll sue you, Howard, for all our expenses as well. It's a clear case of breach of contract. There was no exclusion clause for sickness. Come on, Taylor. We're not here to be gypped. We're going home.'

He flung out of the room, obviously expecting Taylor Marshall to follow him, but the big man stood his ground. There was an odd quality in his stillness, a power that was poised on a knife's edge, ready to be

directed wherever he chose. Jillian held her breath.
There was little to be read from his eyes. He seemed to
be regarding her father sympathetically. When he
spoke it was in a calm, measured tone.

'I'm sorry about your condition, Mr Howard. I
really am. But when Schultzy starts a running play,
I'm afraid I'm bound to follow him until I see where
he's carrying the ball to.' He gave Jillian a courteous
nod. 'Please excuse me, Miss Howard.'

He left, and Jillian's held breath turned into a
deflated sigh. Disappointment was a double-edged
sword. Not only was the charter lost with the direst
consequences, but she had obviously just lost all
attraction to Taylor Marshall. Not that that was
important, but ... She sighed again and met her
father's pained eyes.

'So old George wouldn't do it.'

'No. Sorry, Jilly. You were the only chance left.' He
offered her a travesty of a smile. 'I guess you can't
catch them all. That was one that got away.'

He looked so sick, so beaten, that Jillian could not
bear it. 'They haven't got away from me yet, Dad,'
she said determinedly.

'Oh, Jilly! It's no use. They're probably on their
way back to the airport already.' He tried another
smile. 'Don't you worry, love. I'll be back on my feet
for the next charter. We won't go under.'

Brave, futile words, and they both knew it. Her
father needed the whole season to pay off the new boat
with its ultra-sophisticated equipment. It had been
Jack Howard's dream to run the best possible fishing-
machine, and the success of the last two years had
made it possible. But the payments had to be kept up

and Jillian knew her dress boutique could not meet them. Only a full season's charters could do that.

It would break him, Jillian thought with a sadness that brought tears to her eyes. Her father had given up so much for her, done his best to be both mother and father ever since she had been six years old. She desperately wanted the dream to come true for him. She blinked back her tears and lifted a stubborn chin. The dream was not going to turn to dust if she could help it.

'You're the one who's not to worry, Dad. I won't let them get away that easily. They're not on their way to the airport yet. I've got their luggage locked in the boot of my car, and I'm ready to bait another hook. A Howard never gives up!' And on that determined exit-line, Jillian dropped a kiss on his forehead and scooted out of the room. Adrenalin pumped through her heart at a crazier rate than ever. She had to think of a plan fast. She had to get Taylor Marshall, hook, line and sinker. Somehow. Some way. An inkling of an idea rippled through her mind as she strode through the hospital reception area. There wasn't time to work out the implications. She just had to ride her hunch and roll with his reactions.

They were waiting for her at the car, Earl Schultz puffing on a cigarette and glowering with frustration, Taylor Marshall, casually propped against the bonnet, seemingly unperturbed. The other two men had got out and were standing in aimless poses, their faces long with disappointment.

Jillian strode up to them, exuding a confidence she could not feel. 'I'll drive you on to the hotel now. You must be exhausted after your long trip, and since you won't feel like flying again so soon, tomorrow I'll take you out for a free day's fishing. It's the least we can do for you under the circumstances.'

'What's the catch?' Earl Schultz demanded truculently.

'Only what you're capable of hauling in, Mr Schultz,' Jillian answered breezily, then threw the challenge at Taylor Marshall with a smile which was all stoked up to provoke. A movie star and a top-line football player had to have a very healthy male ego. 'And I'm curious to see if you have what it takes to land a world record, Mr Marshall,' she said sweetly.

His response seemed agonisingly slow in coming. A glint of amusement appeared in his eyes, then tugged at his mouth. Bit by bit a grin spread wide. He began to chuckle and Jillian's taut nerves vibrated to the sound.

'Well, Miss Howard, I must admit I'm curious to see if you've got what it takes as a skipper,' he rolled back at her.

'Taylor, it's just a con,' Earl Schultz snapped.

'Nevertheless I like the idea much better than cramping myself into another aeroplane seat straight away, Earl. I think it's worth spending one day of our lives finding out.' His eyes twinkled a challenge at Jillian. 'And what happens if I land a world record, Miss Howard?'

'You pay for the full charter, Mr Marshall. After all, that was the purpose behind your trip, wasn't it?' she reminded him silkily.

His grin tilted to one side. 'You're very confident.'

'Not at all. Personally, I don't think you have a chance in the world of pulling in the big one. That would take tremendous skill and experience, and I doubt if you have it.' And if that didn't jolt his male ego, nothing would, Jillian thought with mounting desperation.

'Don't you think you're judging without adequate information?' he mocked.

Had she made another mistake? Yet the slight flicker in Taylor Marshall's eyes suggested that he might be niggled. Jillian's smile grew more saccharin as she thrust home her next riposte. 'A habit I picked up from some American acquaintances.'

He threw back his head and gave vent to a full-throated laugh.

'Taylor, it's a waste of time.' Earl Schultz glared his disapproval at Jillian.

She ignored him, concentrating all her will-power on Taylor Marshall, silently begging him to accept the challenge. He, also, ignored his manager, and a wicked mischief danced into his eyes.

'We accept your offer, Miss Howard, on one proviso.'

'And what's that?' she asked, hope surging through her heart.

'That you have dinner with me tonight.'

She hadn't expected that. She looked steadily at him, trying to evaluate the wicked taunt in his eyes. For some inexplicable reason her pulse-rate leapt. Her heart started to sing with elation. 'I'd be delighted to, Mr Marshall,' she said slowly. 'We can talk about fishing.'

'Let's make that Taylor.'

'Jillian,' she responded in kind.

The snort of disapproval from Earl Schultz meant

nothing. The look in Taylor Marshall's eyes was a red-flag warning that he intended to get the better of her, but Jillian knew how to land a big fish. You let him take the bait. Then you played out a tight line and reeled him in.

CHAPTER TWO

NEVER had Jillian's mind been such a powerhouse of activity. She was in with a chance; Taylor Marshall was interested in her. If she played her cards right tonight he might still take the charter, lock, stock and barrel.

She checked back over all of Taylor Marshall's words and actions, jumping ahead to compute her next moves, endlessly revolving around her problem. Having seen the American party safely booked into the Pacific International, she now had four hours left to prepare herself for the dinner date, four hours in which to select the very best bait for Taylor Marshall.

To the city library first, she decided. She had to learn all she could about American football, with specific reference to quarterbacks. A man always liked to talk about his favourite sport, and she could not afford to be ignorant tonight. No possible advantage could be overlooked when the situation was as desperate as this one.

Jillian had no sooner walked into the library than she was thanking God that Cairns was such a cosmopolitan place. Whatever it was . . . the tropical climate, the fascination of the Great Barrier Reef, the easy-paced life . . . people flocked here from all over the world, and so many of them stayed that just about every nationality was well represented. And one of the librarians was an American. Not only an American, but a devotee of the game she had to research. At the mention of Taylor Marshall he poured forth a virtual fount of information. Jillian gleefully took notes.

However, her glow of satisfaction dimmed as she left the library. Apparently Taylor Marshall was an even greater celebrity in America than most movie-stars—and now he was a movie star as well. What chance did she have of capturing the interest of such a man, enough to make him want to stay? About one chance in millions, she thought despondently. About the same chance they had of bringing in a world record marlin.

Even if she hooked up a giant marlin for him tomorrow . . . But what if she didn't? What if they didn't even see a fish tomorrow? It could happen. Even with every other boat in the fleet hauling them in, sometimes the marlin would bypass one boat. There was so much luck involved! No, she couldn't count on the fishing. Which left his interest in her.

A convenient one-night stand . . . that was un-doubtedly how he saw her. A man like him could have his pick of thousands of girls; there was nothing special about her. She was just average-pretty, certainly not spectacular. But thinking negative thoughts was not going to make him stay and take the charter either. Jillian set her chin determinedly. Tonight she would look spectacular, so damned spectacular it would knock his eyes out.

She strode purposefully down the street and into her boutique, only nodding to Pamela who was busy with a customer. She headed straight for the rack which held their selection of evening clothes and, without hesitation, drew out the outfit which had jumped to mind. It was so sexy it was almost indecent. She took one look at it and shook her head. Who was she kidding? It was indecent! Spectacularly indecent. She took it into the changing room.

She had already stripped down to her bikini briefs when Pamela popped her head around the curtain. 'How's your Dad?' she asked in friendly concern.

'In pain and flat on his back, but he'll live,' Jillian tossed at her before lifting the confection of hand-painted silk from its coat hanger.

'Why are you trying that on?'

The surprised note in Pamela's voice brought a grim smile to Jillian's mouth. 'Because I'm going to wear it tonight. If it fits.'

Pamela was dumbstruck. She stood there with her mouth open, eyes wide with shock as Jillian stepped into the skirt, lifted the bodice over her head, and zipped up the skirt. There was not much bodice, only one gathered loop of material which went around her neck, down over her breasts and joined the skirt in devastatingly different places, leaving a three-inch gap of bare skin in between. The white silk was semi-transparent and a hand-painted spray of wattle over each breast hid her nipples but gave provocative interest to the area. The skirt was made of floating panels, the top ones also featuring sprays of wattle. Jillian knew that the skirt was designed to give tantalising glimpses of leg and thigh if she moved, and if she sat . . .

'Holy smoke!' Pamela breathed, then gathered more voice. 'You can't wear that, Jillian. It looks fabulous on you but it's positively dangerous!'

'Exactly!'

Pamela looked bewildered. 'This isn't like you. I've never seen you wear anything other than . . .'

'I've never been so desperate before,' Jillian cut in drily.

'What's wrong?'

Pamela was a good friend but Jillian didn't feel like confiding the whole breadth of the disaster which loomed ahead. 'You're going to have to run the boutique by yourself, Pamela. I don't know for how long. It may be a day, a week, or months. I'm sorry, but it can't be helped. Dad can't get another skipper. I have to do it.'

'Oh my God!'

'It's worse than that, believe you me! Tonight I have to convince the charter who arrived today to stay on, and not sue us for breach of contract.'

Pamela rolled her eyes and shook her head. 'If your father saw you in that dress, he'd smack your bottom, charter or no charter. How are you going to keep the guy's hands off you?'

Jillian took another look at her reflection and nervously fingered the skimpy silk bodice. At least her breasts were large enough and firm enough to hold the material reasonably in place. 'I'll think of something,' she muttered.

'I'd take a machete along,' Pamela suggested with another roll of her eyes. 'I hope you know what you're doing, Jillian.'

So do I, Jillian thought with shivering apprehension as she stripped off the dress. Never in her life had she gone out on a date as a walking, talking invitation for seduction. She wasn't even sexually experienced beyond a little petting. She had met some marvellous guys, but, in a tourist centre like Cairns, they came and went too quickly for any deep emotional involvement to develop, and short-term sex had never appealed to her. How was she going to handle Taylor Marshall if he came on too strong? How would she handle herself? He was so lethally attractive.

The memory of her father's sick, beaten look crawled back into her mind. Resolution stamped on her doubts. What had to be done, had to be done. She just had to be ready for every move Taylor Marshall made and use it to serve her purpose. With renewed determination, Jillian pulled her clothes back on, stuffed the bait-dress into a boutique bag, waved goodbye to Pamela, and shot out into the street before her friend could utter more misgivings.

She was walking along in such a state of mental perturbation that she didn't even see old George until he touched her arm. She jerked away from the contact in instinctive protest, then burst into a torrent of emotional recrimination as he grinned at her.

'How could you refuse Dad when he's in such a terrible bind? You know how much the boat means to him. You know he needs this season.' The tight control that necessity had forced on her suddenly broke, and tears rushed into her eyes. 'I thought we could count on you, George. I really thought you'd come through for us. You've always been...' She shook her head, too distressed to go on.

'Jilly...' He put a comforting arm around her shoulders as she fumbled in her bag for a tissue. 'You can do it, girl. And it's something you should do for your father. You owe it to him, lass. Does a dress shop mean more to you than your father?' he asked in gentle reproof.

'It's not that,' she sniffed. 'They don't think I can do it—the charter.'

'Then you'll just have to prove them wrong,' old George said with smug satisfaction.

Tears welled up again, tears of hopeless frustration. 'You don't understand. I've only got tomorrow to prove myself or they'll call off the charter and go home. They'll sue for breach of contract, George.'

'No!' He was shocked out of his indulgent manner. Anger and concern chased across his face. A grim line settled on his mouth. 'Tomorrow! Damn them for fools! Well, I'll tell you what to do, Jilly. The marlin have been running around Number Ten Ribbon Reef. The boats have all been up there this last week, but the catch wasn't so good today. They'll most likely be at Number Seven Ribbon tomorrow, but that's too far to go for a day trip. Your only chance is deep off Hope Reef. Take my word for it.'

'Please come with me, George,' she begged, instinctively grasping for all the help she could get.

He shook his head. 'Wouldn't do you any good, Jilly, them seeing you look to me for advice. A skipper has to have authority. You know that.'

'But . . .' She made a helpless gesture.

George patted her on the back. 'You know it all, Jilly. You can do it. But if you truly need me for anything, I'll be here for you. Just radio in. OK?'

She nodded resignedly but the desperation in her heart billowed anew.

The old man's eyes peered worriedly at her. 'I wouldn't let you or your Dad down, Jilly. I honestly thought . . .' He heaved a regretful sigh. 'Well, it's done now. But you'll show them, lass. I know you will.'

'Yes,' she choked out. She took a deep, steadying breath and stiffened her spine. 'Thanks for the advice, George. I've got to get going now.'

'You can get me on the radio, Jilly,' he called after her anxiously.

She waved an acknowledgment and fought back more tears. She didn't have time for tears. By this time tomorrow the question of the charter would undoubtedly be settled. Until then all her energy had to be channelled towards getting and keeping Taylor Marshall on a tight line.

As she made the short drive to her home at Holloways Beach, she didn't even see the lush canefields which had drawn the Americans' attention on the way from the airport, nor the numerous clusters of palm trees, nor any of the other tropical attractions. Her mind was on one thing and as soon as she got home she searched out the pertinent contract. It was signed by Taylor Marshall, not by Earl Schultz.

Her inner tension eased a little. She had certainly picked the right man to vamp. Vamp! A hysterical little giggle burst from her throat. Then she recalled just how much of her would be on show tonight and the giggle died. Desperate cases required desperate measures, she told herself firmly.

She telephoned the hospital, told her father about the stay of judgment and assured him that the charter would be all right. Even old George was standing by for her. And for a girl who never told lies, she was getting very good at it, Jillian congratulated herself as she put the telephone down.

She applied herself to studying American football, then applied herself to presenting a spectacular appearance. She washed and blow-dried her long blonde hair into a shining cascade of waves. Her make-up was a masterly piece of understatement; the dress was statement enough. Jillian didn't want to look like a complete tart. She wished her hair reached to her waist instead of only just past her shoulders. The dress made her feel horribly naked.

She experimented with movements in front of the mirror. The peepshow of leg was not too disturbing but the peepshow of breasts was nerve-shaking, and it was utterly impossible to wear a bra, which would be devastatingly obvious. When she leaned over to strap on her high-heeled sandals, her breasts almost popped out of the material. No leaning over, Jillian reminded herself forcefully, and, before her courage could slip, or second thoughts undermine her determination, she grabbed her handbag and left the house.

The eyes of the doorman fairly boggled at her as she entered the huge foyer of the Pacific International. She looked down at her watch, feeling wretchedly self-conscious as other people turned to look at her. It was a minute before seven-thirty. If Taylor Marshall didn't show up in the next sixty seconds she was going to burn up with embarrassment. She cursed herself for being over-punctual. Maybe she could go out and come in again. A set of lift doors opened. She glanced up sharply and felt a confusing welter of emotion as Taylor Marshall stepped out.

He wore a dark grey suit, perfectly tailored to his superb physique, and he looked so absolutely smashing that Jillian didn't have to worry about people looking at her any more : every head turned towards him. But Taylor had eyes only for her. For a moment he seemed stunned. He gave a slight shake of his head and the white, white teeth slowly gleamed into a wolfish grin that curled Jillian's toes. Every step of his approach pounded a wild fear into her heart, and she felt mesmerised by the distinctly predatory gleam in his eyes.

'Wow!'

The explosive breath of appreciation jolted her fuzzy brain. Alarms shrieked around her nervous system. Action stations! 'I'm ... er ... I booked a table at Tawney's for dinner. I think you'll enjoy it there. It's ...' Her voice floundered off. That wasn't what she had meant to say. His gaze was riveted on the valley between her breasts.

'I'm sure I will,' he drawled softly, his meaning all too pointed, then he took her arm and tucked it around his. His eyes smouldered back to hers. 'It's your town, honey. Lead on.'

This was getting far too serious, too fast, Jillian thought fearfully as she led him out of the hotel and across the esplanade. His eyes were drinking in her body movements as they walked, and the warmth emanating from his body was highly disturbing, not to mention the brush of his sleeve against the bare flesh above the side of her waist. She had to do something, say something to distract him. 'Tawney's Restaurant is just over here on the waterfront,' she babbled. 'It overlooks the jetty where our boat is moored and it serves super seafood.'

'Sounds great!' he purred, like a tiger who was eyeing his dinner right now. 'It would be one hell of a shame not to have a good appetite, and I really want you to enjoy yourself tonight, Jillian. So, to save you from being upset or worried I'll give you peace of mind right now.'

She almost sagged against him in relief. He was going to tell her he would accept the charter. He paused beside a tree in the park surrounding the Port Authority building. Elation raced around her veins as he smiled down at her.

'You won't have to spend the whole meal worrying about whether or not I'm going to kiss you later on. I will, but I don't want you to wait that long.'

And before Jillian could reset her mind, his arms were around her and his mouth was on hers, and the whole half-naked length of her body was being pressed to his. Surprise strike, she thought vaguely, and by heaven he was as fast and as powerful and as lethal as a shark. The pressure of his mouth was warm and soft and, after the first stunned moment, Jillian couldn't resist the amazing sensuality of his kiss. No one had ever kissed her like this before, a thorough tasting of her lips, a teasing, tantalising mixture of different pressures, all of them fascinating.

Her skin prickled all over. She was hardly breathing, and the impact of the very masculine body against her barely clad softness almost stopped her thinking. Her arms crept over his shoulders. It was a mistake. Instantly he thrust his body closer to hers and the pressure on her mouth became insistent. Moving in for the kill, she thought dazedly, and the devil of it was, she couldn't afford to resist. Not yet anyway. Relax. Give in, she told herself. He couldn't really mean to make love to her in full view of any passers-by.

She relaxed. And that was a worse mistake. His tongue teased her lips open, then searched out every sensitive nuance of her mouth with a slow eroticism that made chaos of every sensible thought Jillian had ever had. Her hands crept around his neck, instinctively clinging on as he built a crescendo of sensation. Her bare back rippled with sensitivity under the caress of light fingertips. She shivered with pleasure as he delicately fanned the bare flesh from underarm to waist, but when those same fingers edged under her bodice, Jillian was suddenly, intensely aware of her vulnerability. An agitated jerk tore her mouth from his. She gasped for breath. The offending hand moved down, under one of the floating panels of her skirt and over the soft curves of her bottom. It pressed her into a mouth-drying awareness of his sexual arousal.

'Let's postpone dinner,' he murmured, seductively nibbling at her ear.

Her heart gave a frightened leap. Get back in control, her mind shrieked. She pushed some space between them, broke his embrace, and stumbled a few panicky steps away from him before his hands on her arms arrested her escape and swung her back around.

'What are you doing?' he demanded, and the clipped tone held puzzlement and irritation.

She stared at him, bereft of speech. Everything was going wrong. Vamping was supposed to put the woman in control, wasn't it? And she wasn't. She wasn't at all. Anger was starting to smoulder in his eyes. Every scrap of reason told her to offer appeasement—fast! 'It's . . . it's like this, Taylor,' she gasped out, searching her mind for some line to take. 'It's like, in fishing terms, I'm the one that got away.'

Oh God! What had made her say that? He was looking at her in glazed disbelief. Then miraculously he started to smile. Jillian's heart pitter-pattered all over the place. He gave a deep-throated laugh which played havoc with her nervous system.

'Not yet you haven't, honey. Not yet. We'll have our dinner first, and then we'll test how warm the water really is.'

His gaze roved slowly over her, and what he saw apparently convinced him that he was going to have his every desire satisfied before the night was over. Jillian was still trembling from sexual shock . . . or arousal. She was very badly shaken, and his smug, confident air shook her even further.

This plan was going all awry. She needed another, better one, very quickly. She could not afford to offend the man, and in her heart of hearts she didn't want to, but there was no way she could satisfy what he had in mind. She tried desperately to quell her inner panic as they walked on to Tawney's.

It was a relief to enter the restaurant and be amongst other people, even though they were the instant focus of all eyes. To Jillian it was a haven of security, however temporary. They were seated at the window table that she had specified in her booking, and, needing a breathing space from his disturbing gaze, she immediately drew Taylor's attention to the boat bobbing lightly on the water outside.

'That's our fishing machine. It's called *Dream-catcher*. Isn't she a beauty?' she enthused, hoping to get his mind back on to what they should be thinking about.

'I prefer looking at the beauty opposite me,' came the amused reply.

To her intense embarrassment Jillian felt her nipples harden under his wandering gaze. It took all her will-power not to glance down but she fiercely hoped that the sprays of wattle were still in place.

He dragged his gaze back up and smiled. 'I'm afraid I know as much about boats as you know about American football. Fishing is Earl's passion, not mine.'

Oh dear God! She didn't have a hope. But she wasn't giving up. Couldn't give up. A Howard never did. She pasted a bright smile on her face. 'Once you've tried it, you'll never be the same again. It does become a passion...'

'Yes,' he interrupted. 'I agree. You've quite devastated me.'

And he had just cut her feet from under her! Again! Somehow she had to divert him on to another track. Any track! Inspiration was hideously slow in coming, but it came. She smiled. 'I don't believe you. The last time you were really devastated was during a game in Chigaco when you were caught and sacked by Gunnman Perez and Buzz Starr. But you closed the game out in the dying seconds with a pass for an eighty-yard touchdown, which sealed your place in the hall of fame for ever.'

She had to laugh at his stunned expression. Then

he laughed, too, but his eyes were calculating. 'You sure are a fast learner, Jillian.'

'Only trying to keep my head above water,' she retorted lightly, hiding the sheer panic in her heart.

The wine waiter arrived and Taylor ordered champagne without even glancing at the list. Jillian privately vowed to keep her head above that, too. A waitress handed them menus. Jillian stared at hers unseeingly until another plan popped into her mind. She had to play for time. Keep Taylor here as long as possible and then plead an early night because of the fishing trip tomorrow.

Assuming an air of complete sang-froid, Jillian ordered half a dozen oysters, to be followed by the soup of the day, to be followed by smoked salmon, to be followed by the coral trout, and she would order sweets later, thank you. Taylor looked stunned again. He murmured he would have the same and the waitress reluctantly departed, looking equally stunned, though Jillian suspected that Taylor had more to do with that than the meal they had ordered.

'And do all Australian girls have such large appetites?' Taylor asked quizzically.

She was all open-eyed innocence. 'Being out on the water makes you hungry. Be prepared.' How on earth she was going to eat all she had ordered, plus sweets, and a cheese platter, God only knew, but she would force it down somehow.

He eyed her with interested speculation. 'How does a sophisticated girl who runs a dress boutique get to be a skipper?'

'Dad insisted. I go out with him quite a lot. He said if anything ever happened to him I had to be able to bring him home. There's not much to the exam after you've done your sea-time. Mainly local knowledge and a bit of coastal navigation. It's the experience that really counts. I was virtually brought up on a boat.'

'How old are you?'

'Twenty-three. And you?'

'Thirty-two.' His grin teased her. 'Didn't you find that out?'

'I didn't have time for everything. But I wish I did,' she sighed, giving vent to the almost hopeless hope in her heart.

'Well, we have all the time in the world for you to find out all you want tonight,' he drawled, and Jillian was extremely grateful that the lights were low, because she felt her whole body flushing with heat as his gaze once more drifted over her breasts.

Damn him! That wasn't what she had meant at all. She might have captured his interest with this wretched dress but now she had to lift his mind off it.

'Do you enjoy challenges?' she threw at him desperately.

His eyes flicked up and narrowed. 'On the whole, yes, but I like to choose my own challenges. I also like to make my own terms.'

'Then you don't do everything Mr Schultz directs?' she taunted lightly, hoping to prick his male ego again.

He shrugged and gave a little smile that told Jillian he was too self-assured to take that bait too often. 'Earl is paid to push, Jillian. But I only go where I want to.'

'Do you want to leave football and go into films?'

'No. Football comes first. But making a film

amused me. It was a different experience.'

She pounced on the opening. 'Fishing for marlin is a different experience, too.'

She burbled on at high speed, doing her utmost to interest him. And she felt sure she was doing so, right through the oysters and the soup and the smoked salmon and the coral trout, which was made even more delicious by a delicate béarnaise sauce. Then his interest started to flag and he turned the conversation to a more personal level. Quite intimately personal, to her growing discomfort. And his gaze dropped more and more frequently to her breasts as she squirmed in her seat.

'Sure you want the strawberries?' he asked in a tone which was pure bedroom.

'Been looking forward to them all night,' she answered glibly, though it was going to take a Herculean effort to stuff another thing into her mouth.

She switched to talking about American football. It had to be his pet subject and she hoped it would get his mind off her anatomy. It got her through the cheese platter and coffee, then Taylor firmly called for the bill. Butterflies played havoc with the heavy load of food in Jillian's stomach as Taylor lifted her from her chair.

The hand on the small of her bare back, the brush of his jacket sleeve on her naked flesh, aroused goose pimples which had nothing to do with the balmy night air that greeted them as they stepped outside. They walked towards the esplanade while Jillian's mind worked feverishly to produce a casual exit-line. Her brain was positively sluggish, and time ran out.

She stopped Taylor on the hotel corner and offered a grateful smile.

'Thank you for the dinner and a very pleasant evening, Taylor. My car's just across the road. I'll wish you a good night now and be off home. Seven o'clock in the morning, remember?'

He held her arm fast as she tried to move away and his face was a study of perplexity. 'What do you mean, going home?'

Jillian's heart began an accelerated thump but she forced her voice to be calm. 'It's late, Taylor. I have to rise at five o'clock to have the boat ready for you.'

'To hell with the fishing!' he snapped impatiently. 'I want to be with you.'

'Whatever for?' she asked, tugging at her arm to no avail.

'You know what for,' he grated, no honey in his tone at all.

A shaft of light burst into her mind. She smiled. 'But we kissed goodnight before we went to Tawney's. Didn't you notice how it settled my stomach?'

He was grimly unamused. 'Don't give me that nonsense. You've been giving me come-on signals since we met, and if that dress isn't body language I don't know what the hell else you think it is. What are you? Some kind of tease? A pervert who enjoys kicking a man in the groin?'

The accusations chilled her to the bone and shame whispered her reply. 'No. It wasn't that, Taylor.'

'Well, I want some answers, lady, and you can give them to me in my room.'

He had bustled her up the hotel steps before Jillian could protest. 'No, please,' she protested breathlessly, but he shoved her on into the foyer.

'You can make a public display of yourself or come peaceably,' he muttered threateningly, and marched her towards the lifts.

She had no choice. He was seething with anger and if she didn't go with him she could kiss goodbye to the charter. He might not even turn up tomorrow. This wretched dress! She shouldn't have worn it. Jillian suppressed a mounting tide of fear by castigating herself for her stupidity all the way up to the eleventh floor, while Taylor held on to her in grim silence.

He kept an iron grip on her arm right down the corridor and into his room. Then he flung her on to the bed and stood over her, all menacing male frustration. 'Now, tell me without lying, Jillian! Did I read your body language wrong? Are you attracted to me or not?'

'Yes,' she whispered. The breath had practically been knocked out of her.

'Wouldn't you say that the dress you're wearing is provocative?'

Shame burnt into her cheeks, and even with some recovered breath her voice was very small. 'Yes.'

'Designed to encourage a man?'

'Er ... yes.'

'And having done all that, you want to go home?'

'Yes.'

'Why?' he snapped, his eyes so stormy that Jillian tried very hard for an answer to appease.

'I ... I was trying to be a woman of the world. I'm not very good at it yet,' she admitted miserably.

To her astonishment and relief he smiled, but her relief was very short-lived. The smile curled sardonically and his next words punched her heart.

'Then I'll show you, Jillian.'

And before she could register a protest he was on the bed with her, his body pinning her down as his mouth stifled any word she might have spoken. He kissed her without mercy, long, drugging kisses that reduced any protest in Jillian's mind to a weak, formless thing that had no meaning. She felt his hand scoop one of her breasts free from the flimsy silk bodice and, although she clutched at his arm, the sensual expertise of his touch mesmerised her into compliance. He thrust a leg between hers, parting them, and the hard muscularity of his body felt incredibly erotic against her soft womanhood.

He moved, and suddenly his tongue was tantalising her bared nipple and his hand slid under the silk to cup and caress her other breast. She moaned helplessly as a surge of melting pleasure rippled through her body. His other hand pushed under her panties, touching her with such knowing intimacy that Jillian writhed from the exquisite torture, her body bucking between a need for it to stop and a need for it to continue. She was completely lost, inexorably caught up in the sexual heat that Taylor was driving to fever pitch. She had never experienced anything like it before.

Then suddenly he left her. Jillian opened glazed eyes to see him standing up, tearing his shirt off with a haste which spoke of urgent desire. It jolted a little thread of sanity into her mind. He would take her in a matter of moments if she didn't stop him now. But did she want to stop him? He undid his trousers and pushed them down. She had never got this close to sex. Apprehension chilled her own desire. How many times had he done this? With how many women? She would just be another female body to him, a one-night stand! Shame at her own vulnerability writhed through her. Her mind clicked into gear. She had to do something to stop him. But how? He was so much stronger than her.

'Taylor . . .'

He shot a distracted look at her as he bent to tear off his shoes.

How to escape? She needed a moment's diversion. She slid off the bed and stood beside him. 'Taylor, I want to do something to you which you've never had happen before.'

He smiled in dry amusement as his eyes projected plain disbelief that she could do anything that had never happened before, but the sceptical gleam gentled as he sensed her inner tension and he nodded acceptance. 'OK, honey. Anything goes.'

She forced a smile to her lips. 'Will you please turn around. You can watch me in the mirror.'

He turned.

Jillian made it to the door before he realised he had been misled, but he was fast. Even with his trousers still around his ankles he nearly caught her. She slammed the door, virtually in his face, and bolted down the corridor. She punched the 'down' button at the first lift in frantic haste, hearing the thud of footsteps behind her. All her wild prayers were answered when the doors opened instantly. She leapt in and slammed more buttons. Taylor was too late to catch her, but the sight of him, all bristling male aggression in his hastily fastened trousers, was stamped on her memory as the doors closed him out.

With shaking hands, Jillian rearranged her bodice to maximum modesty and had only just finished doing so when the lift halted. On the fifth floor! She had to stand there waiting endless long moments while a party of guests bade farewell to another party, then she had to suffer the interested stares of several strange men as the lift proceeded to the foyer. She was a mass of jangling nerves by the time the doors finally opened to an escape route. She wanted to run, but she forced herself to walk until she was out of the hotel. Then she ran. She was almost to her car when she heard the footsteps pounding after her. She threw a fearful glance over her shoulder.

Taylor Marshall! Oh God! Please God, help me, she begged, trying to thrust the key into the door lock. He was still bare-chested and bare-footed, but the bared muscular torso only increased his menace. Even in the dim glow of the street light his face looked thunderous.

The door lock turned. Jillian snatched out the key, wrenched open the door and leapt into the driving seat, slamming the door behind her and locking it. Just in time! Taylor thumped the window demandingly. She met his murderous eyes and knew he was never going to forgive her. Everything had gone hopelessly out of control. With a heavy heart she wound down the window an inch.

'I'm sorry, Taylor. I couldn't stay.'

'You bitch of a liar!' he grated furiously.

Tears of mortification rushed to her eyes. 'I'm sorry, Taylor,' she choked out. 'No matter what the cost, I couldn't do it.'

The tears trickled down her cheeks. Taylor glared at her, gave a snarl of disgust, then stepped back. He sliced a hand back at her in dismissal, turned, and, with a back stiff with resentment, strode away.

Sicker at heart than she had ever been, Jillian started the engine and drove off, not looking back at the man she had unwittingly driven to such terrible anger. Total despair blacked out her mind. She had surely cut the line which it had been so necessary to keep intact.

CHAPTER THREE

IT was already five minutes past seven and there was no sign of them. They weren't coming, Jillian concluded. A wave of misery brought tears to her eyes but she blinked them away. She couldn't give way yet. She had no real hope that the Americans would turn up, but if by some miracle they did, it would hardly be appropriate for her to be found howling her eyes out. If they didn't come, she would probably go home and commit suicide.

It was her own wretched fault, Jillian thought despairingly. She had made such a fool of herself last night, completely blown any chance they might have had. The look of hostility on Taylor Marshall's face ... The memory made her shudder. She couldn't blame him for not turning up, for not wanting to turn up. But if only he would, she would show him a different Jillian Howard. She would do her utmost to earn his respect.

Another five minutes ticked by. 'They're late,' Bob muttered, scanning the length of the jetty yet again.

Jillian lifted bleak eyes to her father's number one deckie. Bob Tanner had been with her father for three years now and Jack Howard declared him the best deckie ever: smart, efficient, responsible, and the keenest eye around. He was twenty-nine, short but immensely strong, and his sunny personality quickly endeared him to their charters. His blue eyes sparkled with friendliness, his homely face always looked good-humoured, and his mop of sun-bleached yellow hair was testament to his years at sea.

But not even Bob's ready cheerfulness had been able to lift Jillian's spirits this morning. Anxiety had continued to eat into her heart even as they did all the chores in preparation for the day's fishing. The refrigerator and bar were re-stocked, the boat was spotless, the Dacron fishing lines checked for any form of fraying, baits made up, bilge-water emptied, valves opened for the diesel and water supplies; all shipshape and ready to go. Except the charter had not turned up, and Jillian was at a complete loss as to what to do, once the full extent of the disaster could no longer be denied.

'Here they come!' Bob called, and Jillian's heart did a somersault.

Bob was halfway up the ladder to the jetty before her mind could override her leaping pulse enough to even think, let alone order some action. How was she going to face Taylor Marshall after last night? What could she even say to him? She snatched up her Polaroid glasses and shoved them on, instinctively hiding behind them just as she had instinctively hidden her body under baggy jeans and a loose checked shirt earlier this morning.

She tried very hard to control her agitation as she walked out of the cabin to the fishing cockpit where all the action would take place today. God willing! Taylor Marshall was giving her another chance. That was the only fact of importance.

She gripped on to the back of the fighting-chair to steady herself and listened to the Americans' voices as they responded to Bob's cheery chatter ... Jerry Somers pleasant, Gordon Duffy keen with anticipation, Earl Schultz surly, Taylor Marshall very neutral, almost expressionless. So all four had come, Jillian thought with a sharp twinge of relief.

The boat rocked as the men boarded. Jerry Somers was the first along the deck, carefully manoeuvring a large camera case. He used the observer's seat to step down to Jillian's level, watching his footing as if he had never been on a boat before.

'Welcome aboard, Mr Somers,' Jillian said brightly.

He did a slight double-take at her appearance, which was in sharp contrast to yesterday's sophistication. Apart from her workmanlike clothes, Jillian was not wearing any make-up and her ponytail was positively juvenile, but it was performance, not appearance, that would count today. If anything counted. And if she could perform.

Gordon Duffy came next. He politely returned her greeting but was instantly on the move, keenly eyeing the fishing equipment. Earl Schultz jumped down impatiently, casting a critical glance around even while mumbling a disgruntled response to her welcome. Jillian desperately wanted to look away as Taylor Marshall appeared but she steeled herself to greet him too. He was in shorts and T-shirt, his very male physique all too disturbingly obvious, and his expression was totally enigmatic. He nodded acknowledgment at her but showed no reaction to her change of image. There was a cold reserve in his eyes which chilled her to the bone.

'Why haven't you got the engines warmed up?'

Earl Schultz demanded truculently. 'We're late as it is.'

Jillian disciplined the antagonism he aroused in her. Today she had to keep control at all costs. 'It's not my fault you're late, Mr Schultz. As for the engines, today I'm paying for the fuel, and it's too costly to waste by marking time at a jetty.' Having answered the criticism, Jillian steeled herself to meet Taylor Marshall's eyes again. 'I'd like to make a few points clear before we start.'

'I'd appreciate that,' he drawled with a touch of derision.

A painful flush burnt into Jillian's cheeks but she gritted her teeth and crushed the memory of last night. That was past. This was another day. 'It will take some time to reach the fishing grounds. While we're on our way, Bob will put you through a practice session of getting into the seat harness. You'll need to . . .'

'Seat harness? What are you talking about?' Earl Schultz cut in impatiently. 'I've always used a shoulder harness.'

'You may use a shoulder harness if you wish to, Mr Schultz, but I don't recommend it,' Jillian said with all the authority she could muster. She turned her attention back to Taylor. He was the man she had to convince. 'To hold a giant marlin on the line you'll need to use the strength of your whole body, not just your shoulders, and this fighting-chair is designed for that purpose. You brace your legs against the foot rest, and Bob will adjust the back of the chair to suit whoever's taking the strike.'

She drew in a sharp breath and continued. 'The

International Game Fishing Association does not recognise a record claim if anyone but the angler touches the rod, so no one can help you once the hook-up is called. You'll have about four seconds to get into the chair, put the harness on, and lift the rod from its slot in the armrest to the gimbal over the centre of the chair. It needs practice. The faster you are, the better.'

Taylor's expression had been completely impassive throughout her long lecture, and Jillian's nerves were stretched to screaming pitch by the time she had finished. If he went against her she might as well give up now.

He slowly nodded. 'Then we'll practise.'

Her relief was short-lived. Earl Schultz was displeased. He picked on Bob. 'You there, you'll be taking your orders from Gordon today.'

Jillian had never seen Bob anything less than good-humoured, but the insult hit his pride. He turned to her in a silent but very sharp demand for her support. She looked back at Earl Schultz, took in the meanly narrowed eyes, the stubborn tilt of his chisel chin, and knew that if she refused he would more than likely walk off the boat. But a skipper had to have authority. All that she had ever been taught rebelled against Earl Schultz's edict. Her voice shook a little as she stated her own, necessary position.

'I have to disagree, Mr Schultz. They will both take their orders from me.'

His thin mouth thinned even further. 'Either I call the shots or we call the day off.'

Anger drowned her apprehension. This was her father's boat and it was her responsibility. Earl

Schultz wouldn't have been so damned arrogant with Jack Howard, Jillian thought mutinously, but she was the skipper today and skipper she would be! Any charter would be impossible if she did not assert her authority right here and now. 'It's your prerogative to call the shots in the fishing, Mr Schultz, but the overall responsibility for the safety of everyone on board is mine.'

She flashed a steely look at Taylor Marshall who was now wearing a grimly amused smile. And damn him, too! She hadn't set out to frustrate him last night. 'When you play football, Mr Marshall, who calls the plays? The coach or the quarterback?' she flung at him defiantly.

For the first time since he had come on board something flickered across the cold reserve in his eyes. 'Mostly the coach,' he answered softly.

'That's different!' Earl Schultz snapped.

Taylor eyed Jillian for a moment longer, then switched his gaze back to his manager. 'Nevertheless, I think we'll go along with Miss Howard, Earl. After all, she is paying for the pleasure she's giving us.'

The edge of sarcasm in that last comment cut through Jillian like a knife, but at least he had come down on her side, she consoled herself.

'You trust her judgment?' Earl Schultz snarled, with scornful emphasis on the 'her'.

'In this particular field of expertise, I have no reason not to,' Taylor answered evenly, then sliced a narrowed look at Jillian as he added, 'yet.'

Inwardly she squirmed at the pointed reminder of last night's fiasco, but pride forced her chin to lift above it. 'Thank you. Now that we have that settled, we'll get moving. Please excuse me. I'll go up and start the engines. Bob, get ready to cast off.'

'Ay, ay, skipper.' He beamed at her, a great grin all over his face.

Bob's vote of confidence did not restore Jillian's equilibrium. She was trembling as she climbed the ladder to the fly-bridge, her nerves shredded from the effort of exerting control for a few minutes, let alone for twelve hours. It was surely going to be a dreadful day. The task of convincing Taylor Marshall and Earl Schultz to keep on the charter seemed even more impossible, and as for any plan at all, her mind was a complete blank.

The engines started with a great growl and she let them run for a minute or two before signalling Bob to cast off the mooring line. Using the throttles of both engines, Jillian cautiously manoeuvred the fifty-foot boat away from the jetty. Normally her father did this and she wasn't very experienced. The last thing she needed to do was to show incompetence by bumping the boat into a pier. Having negotiated that hurdle without incident, she expelled a long sigh of relief and steered for the ten-mile channel out of Cairns. She switched on the depth-sounder. The channel needed constant dredging and, while it was easy to follow, Jack Howard had impressed on her since childhood that every precaution must be taken on a boat.

Once the engines were warmed up Jillian eased the throttles open. The seven-hundred horsepower motors responded with a surge of speed which was exhilarating. *Dreamcatcher* ploughed through the water, sending up a huge white bow wave. The powerful throb of the boat, the sensation of cleaving through the water, the brisk air and the smell of sea, all combined to ease Jillian's physical tension, but her mind was a mire of black thoughts.

It could only be curiosity about marlin fishing that had brought Taylor Marshall out today. Logic told her that he could not want anything to do with her, not in any personal way, not after last night, and the terrible truth was that she felt more attracted to him than ever. He was almost irresistible. Heat suffused her body as she remembered her response to him last night. She almost wished she had given in to him. It would have been so easy to let it happen, to have him as he had wanted to have her. And then ...

Jillian wrenched her traitorous mind off that spine-tingling speculation. She should be worrying about the charter, yet common sense kept getting overshadowed by a host of womanly instincts which were all zeroed in on Taylor Marshall's reaction to her. It was stupid and irrational, but she couldn't help it.

Michaelmas Cay was looming up on the horizon when she felt the presence of someone behind her. The hopelessness of any future with Taylor Marshall, no matter how short, had distracted her so deeply that she hadn't heard anyone climbing the ladder. Her body gave a startled jerk when her lateral vision picked up Taylor. Her heart began an agitated pounding when he slid on to the bench-seat to her left. She just couldn't feel normal at all when he was near her. Why had he come up here? To taunt her? To abuse her for last night's idiocy?

'Great sensation!'

She flicked him a glance in an attempt to gauge what the words meant, if they were an oblique reprimand for her behaviour last night, but it seemed he was only making an innocuous comment about the speed of the boat. He wasn't even looking at her. And she felt positively dizzy from looking at him. She tried desperately hard to get her head in order.

'We're doing over thirty knots an hour,' she told him, while telling herself sternly that she was way out of his league, and the sooner she accepted that, the better for her peace of mind.

'Is that an island ahead?'

Grateful for any form of communication with him, Jillian spouted forth information. 'No, it's a coral cay, part of the reef that's above water. You'll see thousands of birds nesting on it as we pass. Officially it's a bird sanctuary.'

'The sand is very white,' he observed.

She hesitated to correct him. She could detect no hostility in his tone and she didn't want to raise any. If by some miracle he was offering a peace-line of conversation, she didn't want to discourage him either. 'It's not really sand. It's ground up coral,' she stated matter-of-factly.

The ensuing silence from him was agonising to Jillian. A sideways glance showed him looking ahead to the cay but there was too much guilt and shame on her mind for her to dismiss last night and simply accept the fascination and excitement of his presence.

'Taylor ... about last night ... I'd ... I'd like to apologise,' she got out in a squirm of embarrassment.

'So you should. If that's the way you carry on when your father is laid up, the sooner he gets out of hospital, the more peaceful it will be for all the male population of Cairns.'

The flat, unemotional statement gave her no forgiveness and she deperately wanted his forgiveness. And not entirely for the sake of the charter. She needed Taylor Marshall to think well of her. 'I . . . I did the wrong thing,' she stammered while floundering for more suitable words.

'Forget it,' Taylor said irritably, then in a tone of dry irony added, 'I find it eminently forgettable.'

Jillian winced. She knew she would never forget her own response to him but no doubt he had enjoyed the company of hundreds of girls who had given him more pleasure, plus the sexual satisfaction she had run from. She should be grateful for the forbearance he was showing at the moment, and she was grateful in her mind, but her emotions could find no joy in it. She was less than nothing to him now. Eminently forgettable.

But maybe the fishing trip would not be so dreadful, and maybe, just maybe, if he held no grudge against her, he might still accept the charter, and then she would have a fortnight of his company. Hope stirred anew. Suddenly it was all the more important that today she change his mind about staying on. A fortnight could be a lifetime to her.

'Bob was showing us a map of the reefs,' he remarked conversationally. 'There are a mighty lot of them. It must take a great deal of skill to steer a safe course. Have you ever run aground?'

'Not yet.' She slanted him a wry smile. 'It's a saying here that there are only two kinds of skippers: those that have hit the reef and those that are going to.'

His grin was wonderfully rewarding. A squeamish thrill of happiness raced around Jillian's veins. She wanted him to look like that all the time he was with her. If only she could make him happy. She wished . . . Oh, she wished she could have last night all over again. If only she had been her natural self with him.

'Has your father hit it?' he asked curiously.

'Yes. A couple of times.' She had to grin at his surprise. Apparently he hadn't expected a lead skipper to err in any way. 'But Dad's too good a skipper to have hit so hard as to damage the boat. Only a couple of scrapes really,' she added in mitigation.

To Jillian's increasing sense of pleasure, Taylor stayed with her all the way to Hope Reef, seemingly fascinated by the radar equipment and the colour digital sounder which showed up everything between the ocean floor and the boat. Jillian enjoyed showing off her knowledge and Taylor seemed impressed by it, but she knew her knowledge would count for nothing if she didn't hook up a marlin today.

Tension started twanging along her nerves as they reached the fishing grounds beyond Hope Reef. She throttled down the engines and leaned over the railing to call to Bob, 'Pass me up my belt and fix the outriggers! We'll start trolling!'

'What's the purpose of those?' Taylor asked as he watched the long poles swing out to be fixed at right angles to the boat.

'The lines are attached to the tips. It keeps the baits apart, and when a fish strikes, the extra loop of line attached to the outrigger snaps out and gives you a few vital seconds to get into the chair,' she explained as she buckled her belt on.

'And why the belt?'

'It has wire-cutters and pliers attached to it. A

skipper doesn't have to wear a belt but the deckies do, and Dad insists that the skipper should, too. Dad maintains that everyone should be ready for an emergency.' She hesitated, then added reluctantly, 'You'd better go down, Taylor. No telling when a marlin will hit and you'll need to be on the spot.'

He didn't move. 'I told Earl to take the first one. I want to watch the action before I try my hand at it.'

The first one! They'd be lucky to get one hook-up, let alone two! Jillian chopped down on the pessimistic thought and scanned the water as Bob and Gordon put the baits out. She hoped Bob had checked Gordon's bait. She had no confidence in Earl Schultz's deckie. He might be all right but his lack of experience with the black marlin did not encourage confidence.

The strain of the next hour took the edge off her pleasure in Taylor's company. Two baits were ruined by wahoo, big eighty-pound fish which tore through the water, chomping the tuna-bait in half on their way, without even touching the hook. Each time the line had snapped out, Earl Schultz had leapt into the chair, only to be doubly frustrated as Jillian called out what had happened. She noticed that Gordon was far slower than Bob in rebaiting his line and she seethed with impatience at the unnecessary delay.

'Just remember I'll be calling the shots when we do get a hook-up,' Earl Schultz growled at her the second time he was disappointed.

Another hour passed and Jillian's eyes ached from endlessly searching the water for any sign of marlin. Despite her intense concentration it was Bob who saw it first.

'Fish up!'

Her hands instantly took hold of the controls. Adrenalin pumped through her heart as her eyes followed Bob's pointing finger to the flash of blue and silver streaking through the water towards the bait. It was a marlin, all right, and it took the bait, hard and fast. She waited the fraction of time necessary for the bait to be fully swallowed, then hit the throttles full bore, even before Earl Schultz screamed, 'Go!'

The hook bit and stuck. The marlin came out of the water, its huge streamlined body an iridescent blue, black pectoral fins flashing against the sky, its spear-like bill thrashing from side to side in a fight to throw the hook.

'My God!' It was a breath of wonder from Taylor, but Jillian had no time to give him the attention she would have liked. She had her hands full, controlling the boat.

Earl Schultz had himself well braced in the chair, pumping the rod with an experienced action. 'Back up! Back up!' he yelled.

It was the wrong move; Jillian knew it instinctively. She had seen fish lost like this before. The marlin was coming towards them. The way it was throwing its head, it could corkscrew the wire around its bill if there was any slack line. Despite the strength of the thirty feet of wire between the hook imbedded in the fish and the Dacron line to which it joined, if it tangled with a marlin's bill, that was the end of it.

'Back up!' Earl Schultz screamed, reeling in as fast as he could.

She had no choice. He had insisted on calling the shots! Jillian hit reverse and backed up. The huge fish walked along the water on its tail, its body whiplashing in its bid to rid itself of the hook. Earl reeled in like a madman but he wasn't fast enough. Jillian's fear was realised all too soon. The wire broke and the marlin was off, leaping across the water in what seemed like a triumphant dance of freedom, and a slap in the face for the angler.

'Goddammit!' Earl Schultz cursed as he got out of the chair and glared up at Jillian. 'You let it get away!'

The charge of incompetence in front of Taylor could not be borne. The loss of the fish was not her fault. If an angler wanted to call the shots, it was his job to call them right. She squared her back and gave Earl Schultz a shot of the truth, straight between the eyeballs. 'Mr Schultz, you ordered me to back up. You called the shots. My choice would have been to take the boat around in a loop to prevent the marlin from corkscrewing the wire.'

'Corkscrew?'

Bob had pulled the line in and he held out the curled wire for Earl Schultz to see while he took over the explanation. 'A marlin's bill is strong enough to break just about anything. So strong it'll go through two feet of wood or four inches of steel. Get this around its bill and snap! Every time.'

Earl Schultz muttered something under his breath, then shot a look at Gordon Duffy. 'How big was it?'

'Around seven hundred pounds, I reckon,' came the cautious answer.

'Damn!' Earl muttered, but he threw no more criticism at Jillian.

'Get that line back in the water as fast as you can, Bob,' she ordered, and turned away to get the boat trolling again, chagrin biting into her heart. They had had their chance and Earl Schultz had blown it. And blown the last vestige of hope for the charter. Two big marlin in one day was asking too much of Fate. 'You'd better go down now, Taylor,' she grated. 'I wouldn't want you to miss out.' If Fate was phenomenally kind!

He nodded and stood up. 'If you hook me up a fish, Jillian, don't take a damned bit of notice of anything Earl says. Do what you think is best. And I'll do my best to follow all advice.'

His vote of confidence eased some of the pain of disappointment and the kind note in his voice brought tears to her eyes. But she didn't want kindness from him. She wanted . . . Oh God! She had to get another hook-up! If he experienced the thrill of catching a marlin he might stay on. He just might!

She trolled for another hour with no luck. Bob served lunch. Another fruitless hour passed. Earl Schultz was becoming restless, impatient with the lack of action, and still frustrated by his own lost opportunity. Jillian was deeply plunged into despair when a line snapped out of the outrigger.

'Fish on reel two!' she yelled, gunning the motors to get the hook-up. The line screamed out of the reel while Taylor was getting settled into the chair.

'Come on! Come on!' she urged. She had only seen a flash of the fish as the bait was taken but it had looked big and it was travelling fast. She breathed a tortured sigh of relief as Taylor fixed the rod in the gimbal and leaned back, achieving the vital tension on the line. He struck hard and the marlin climbed out of the water, huge, majestic, fighting!

'She's a big mother!' Bob hooted with excitement.

No doubt about it, Jillian thought with elation. Only females grew to that size and it was at least a thousand pounds, maybe more.

Gordon Duffy, Earl Schultz and Jerry Somers were all standing thunderstruck at the incredible spectacle of a giant marlin in action. Then Earl Schultz was hurling orders at Jerry Somers and the cameraman snapped out of his daze.

'Backing up now, Taylor. Keep the tension!' she rapped out, and watched with satisfaction as he reeled in every bit of slack she gave him. Several times the marlin leapt, performing heart-stopping acrobatics as it tried to throw the hook. But it held. The fish sped away on a long run. Jillian kept the boat within tight range. The marlin went deep. Jillian put the boat into a repeated circling pattern, pressuring the fish to rise again. Bob yelled advice at Taylor, keeping him working at lifting, leading, forcing the fish to change direction, to come back to the top.

Jillian found it increasingly difficult to keep her mind on the job. Her eyes were drawn to Taylor again and again. Every muscle of his superb body was stretched taut, glistening with perspiration. The sheer animal strength of the man awed her, and whenever he moved it was with the quick grace and sure co-ordination of an athlete in top condition. And she remembered the way his body had moved over hers last night. The thought of all that vital masculinity against her, as taut as it was now, as urgent as . . .

The marlin came out of the water in a huge leap and Jillian almost leapt with it. Her mind whipped

back on to the job in hand. The fish was streaking off
again, but not quite so fast this time. It was weakened.
Taylor's action with rod and reel had become very
smooth throughout the long fight, and now, under
Bob's coaching, he began to bring the fish in, co-
ordination, concentration and good timing all evident
in the fluid motion of pumping the rod and reeling in
the line. At first it was only inches of line being
recovered with each pump, but gradually it became
feet, and the giant marlin was inexorably drawn
closer and closer.

Elation bubbled through Jillian as the leader wire
dripped out of the water. The marlin was only thirty
feet behind the wire. Surely Taylor had to feel
exhilarated at bringing in such a catch. The fight had
gone on for some ninety minutes and he had met the
challenge all the way. Jillian sensed he was close to
exhaustion but victory was only a few minutes away
now, and the fight had definitely provided all the
excitement that Jillian could have asked as a persuad-
er for Taylor to accept the charter. If this didn't work,
nothing would.

Gordon Duffy moved into position to take hold of
the leader wire and only then did Jillian recall that he
had been responsible for the number two line all day.
She suffered a twinge of uncertainty as to his ability to
haul the fish in safely, but Bob was already busy with
the gaff-rope so she held her tongue. Until Gorden
Duffy reached for the wire. He was wearing only one
pair of gloves. Jillian's blood ran cold. He hadn't
pulled on the cotton outer gloves which were so
necessary for handling the wire. If the fish made a run
for it at the last minute . . .

'Get your outers on, Gordon!' she shouted in sharp urgency.

'It's OK,' he threw back, ignoring her order. 'I've done it before.'

'It's not OK! Get them on!'

He grabbed the wire and started hauling it in, winding it around his hand in the usual practice.

'Bob, take the wire from him!' she snapped out.

Too late! The sight of the boat sent the fish off in a last despairing bid for freedom. Gordon screamed as the wire cut behind the leather inserts of his gloves, fixing him securely to the line. As if in slow motion, Jillian watched as the deckie was effortlessly plucked from the cockpit, pulled over the stern and into the water. Bob leapt after him. Even as it all happened Jillian reacted instinctively, swinging the boat to protect Gordon from the propellers, throwing the throttles into neutral to stop the blades revolving.

She yelled at the men to throw out a rope as she swiftly discarded her jeans. A leap on to the top railing, then she was diving the twelve feet into the water. Only she and Bob had the wire-cutters that could save Gordon from drowning; he had to be cut free from the marlin. Even as she hit the water her hands were scrabbling at her belt for the necessary tool. Her eyes searched desperately for a sight of either man or marlin. She kicked a wide circle in a futile search, then had to break surface to ease her bursting lungs.

She swept a frantic look around and breathed a sigh of relief. Bob had him! The next moment both men were sinking again. Gordon was writhing in Bob's hold, fighting him in panic. Or in pain, Jillian thought grimly, and struck out in their direction, kicking with all the strength of her long legs. She reached them in time to help Bob lift the struggling man to air again. With her extra support Bob was able to swing back one arm and deliver a knock-out punch to Gordon's chin. The injured deckie went limp. Bob and Jillian towed him to the boat as fast as they could. Taylor Marshall threw them a rope. Bob grabbed it and Taylor hauled them in.

'Open the transom door,' Jillian yelled and fortunately Earl Shultz knew what she meant for he immediately moved to the stern of the boat. It was the door through which big fish could be brought into the cockpit, and it was the best way to get Gordon back on board. The cut wire was still around his hand and it looked ominously deep.

'Don't touch his hand 'til I get some advice on it,' she commanded, as Taylor and his manager lifted Gordon from the water.

She scrambled into the cockpit after him, racing for the radio as soon as she was on her feet. She called the seaplane, spelling out the emergency with an urgency that asked for and was given a promise of immediate service. The plane was actually operating in the area and within five minutes Jillian spotted it. Bob had wrapped Gordon in blankets while she was on the radio and there was nothing else she could do for the man who was now moaning in agony. She helped Bob get the dinghy in the water.

'How many passengers does the plane take?' Taylor asked her in sharp concern. 'I think we should go with Gordon if we can. See him to the hospital and get the best treatment for him.'

There was room for them in the plane and they all went. Jillian watched the plane take off with utter despair in her heart. She felt sorry for Gordon Duffy but she bitterly resented him, too. But for his inexperience and refusal to obey orders, she would have nailed the charter with Taylor's marlin. Although the failure had to sit on her shoulders, too, she acknowledged miserably. More on hers than on Gordon's. It was her responsibility to ensure the safety of everyone on board. She should have hammered in the necessity of wearing the cotton gloves that could be so easily discarded if the fish ran, especially so when she had known that Gordon was inexperienced with giant marlin.

In a terrible weariness of spirit she fetched her jeans and went into the cabin to change out of her wet clothes. She pulled on one of the boat's T-shirts with *Dreamcatcher* emblazoned across the chest. Only shattered dreams today, she thought despairingly. Respectably and drily clothed, she helped Bob stow the dinghy back on board, then climbed up to the fly-bridge once more to head the boat for home. Bob did all the cleaning up below then joined her on the bridge, as low in spirits as herself.

'I told him. I gave him the outers and told him why they had to be worn,' Bob said in mournful exasperation. 'I should have kept my eye on him. You told me to.'

'It's not your fault, Bob,' Jillian soothed. 'It's mine. You know it is, so don't blame yourself for anything. You did your job and more.' She threw him a wobbly but grateful smile. 'Thanks for saving him. I doubt that I'd have caught him.'

'You did fine, Jilly!' he insisted loyally. 'As good a skipper as your father any day. I felt like giving that Earl Schultz a knuckle sandwich but you handled him great! Taylor Marshall was a good guy though. I liked him. It's a damned shame that . . .' Bob heaved a regretful sigh and didn't bother recalling the grim end to the day.

It sat heavily on both their minds all the way back to Cairns. Jillian didn't know how she was going to face her father and tell him what had happened. That was bad enough, but she knew that the pain in her heart was related more to the loss of Taylor than the loss of the charter.

'So what happens now?' Bob asked as they walked along the jetty.

'I don't know, Bob. I'll have to go and see Dad. I'll let you know as soon as I can.'

'Reckon I'll go and sink a few beers in the Marlin Bar. I'll be there if you need me, Jilly.'

She thanked him and waved him off, thinking how much she'd like to drown her woes in a haze of alcohol, but not even a thousand beers could make them disappear, or give her what she wanted. She dragged her feet over to her car and sank into the driver's seat. It was some time before she could force herself to start the engine, and even then she just about crawled to the hospital, postponing the inevitable as long as possible.

She enquired about Gordon at the reception desk and was informed that he would be undergoing micro-surgery on his fingers as soon as possible. She could do nothing for him. A visit was pointless; he was under sedation. As far as the receptionist knew, the rest of the American party had returned to their hotel.

Jillian went up to her father's room, knowing that her news would give him more pain than his physical condition. It seemed horribly ironic that he should meet her doleful gaze with a sympathetic look. She gave a helpless shrug 'I'm sorry, Dad. I messed up.'

He stretched out a hand to her. 'You did your best, Jilly, and from what I hear, your best was pretty good,' he said gently.

She took his hand and pressed it as she gave him a wry smile. 'From what you hear? Has the hospital grapevine already reached you about Gordon Duffy?'

'No. Taylor Marshall came to see me. He's just left as a matter of fact. And I'm very proud of you, Jilly. Very proud.'

His eyes were moist as he delivered his fatherly accolade, and Jillian was so deeply moved she could not speak. She squeezed his hand, blinked tears from her own eyes and swallowed hard.

'But ... but I lost the charter,' she choked out.

'No, you didn't, Jilly. You won it. Won it with your skill and bravery. And no man could ever have felt prouder of his daughter than I felt, as Taylor Marshall spoke of how you handled yourself today. The charter stands and so do you as skipper, Jilly.'

A tumult of emotion swept through her. She sank on to the chair beside her father's bed, suddenly too weak to remain standing. She shook her head in disbelief. 'Are you sure, Dad? He really said he'd keep the charter on?'

'With you as skipper,' Jack Howard repeated with happy relish and a huge grin banished any greyness from his face. 'So you'd better get going, Jilly. There's a lot to be done before you go out on the water for a two-week stretch.'

'Yes!' Two weeks! Two weeks with Taylor Marshall! She jumped to her feet again, fired by an amazing burst of energy. She grinned back at her father then leaned over and kissed him exuberantly. 'Thanks, Dad. You look after yourself now.'

'Good luck, Jilly,' he said huskily. 'Best daughter a man ever had.'

'That's because she has the best Dad,' Jillian retorted, and virtually skipped out of his room, riding on a high that was filled with thoughts of Taylor Marshall.

What a marvellous man! What a simply beautiful, marvellous man! And to her absolute delight, the marvellous man was leaning on the bonnet of her car when she came out of the hospital. He smiled at her, really smiled at her, and all her insides melted into a warm yearning. It was more than attraction, more than wanting, but Jillian had no time to stop and define her feeling. Taylor Marshall was waiting for her.

CHAPTER FOUR

As she walked towards Taylor, Jillian fiercely wished she had done something to tidy up her appearance before she had left the boat. She had been too upset to even think of combing her hair, and it still hung in salty rats' tails from her dive into the sea. Taylor's gaze dropped momentarily to the *Dreamcatcher* emblem on her T-shirt and she flushed with embarrassment, recalling that she had discarded her wet bra along with her wet shirt.

But there was no teasing, nothing at all provocative in the warm brown eyes that met hers. 'You've seen your father?' he asked softly.

'Yes,' she breathed, then tried to force a sensible level to her voice. 'He said you're taking the charter.'

He nodded. 'I waited to thank you personally for what you did today.'

She squirmed under his open admiration. 'Any skipper would have done the same thing.'

'I don't know about that, but for fast reflexes and effective action I'd have you on my team any time. Will you be able to replace Gordon with a local deckie? At my expense, of course,' he added quickly, seeing her frown.

All the best deckies were booked up for the season. Even her father's number two deckie, Terry Lewis, had been snapped up by another skipper for the duration of this charter. 'It'll be difficult, but Bob will probably know someone,' she said slowly, then smiled reassurance. 'We'll manage somehow. Bob is so good he only needs a helpmate.'

Taylor returned a wry smile. 'He sure is. It opened Earl's eyes to see the speed and skill with which he baited those hooks. Gordon took twice the time. And speaking of Gordon, Earl will stay here tomorrow to see him through the operation. Then he'll fly out to the mother-ship with our luggage. So it'll only be Jerry and me tomorrow, and we'll be on the boat, seven o'clock sharp.' He grinned a friendly open grin. 'You can have the engines warmed up ready to go.'

'I'll do that,' she grinned back at him, and was still standing there grinning after him while he strolled half a block and turned the corner in the direction of the hotel. Then she castigated herself for mindless stupidity. She should have offered him a lift. She should have ... Too late now, she sighed. But tomorrow was another day—and then there were twelve more days.

Elation bubbled through her again. She jumped into the car and drove down to the Great Northern Hotel, determined that everything would go right for the rest of the charter. The Marlin Bar was crowded, as it usually was at this time of day. The dim light was made dimmer by a fug of smoke, and conversation was boisterous with stories of the day's catch. Jillian found Bob with old George and suddenly she had the answer to every possible problem. Her smile was positively radiant as she regarded the two men. 'Bob, the charter is on. Are all the stores on the boat?'

'Ready to go,' he beamed at her. 'That's great, Jilly!'

Jillian fixed old George with commanding eyes. 'Drink up, old-timer, because that's the last whisky you're having for a long time. You're going to be skipper of *Dreamcatcher* from tomorrow on, until the season ends.'

He settled back in his chair with the air of a man who was never going to move. 'Nope! Too much responsibility, lass. I even hear that these days the skipper has to go diving into the water to rescue the crew.'

'You promised, George. You said you'd be here if I needed you and I need you. If you're not on the boat by six-thirty tomorrow, I'm coming after you with a gaff. I can do the work of a second deckie but I need you to be the skipper. The next two weeks will be the greatest charter ever worked off the north coast and I intend *Dreamcatcher* to be the lead boat by a record margin at the end of the season, and for that to happen, George, we need your expertise.'

He snuffled in his beard, worked his lips as if in some indecision, then crinkled his eyes at her. 'You've made your mind up on that, Jilly?'

'Sure have, George.'

He shrugged. 'Guess I'll have to come with you then.'

Elation shone into her smile. 'Thanks, George.'

He grinned. 'Except that I'm going to be the second deckie. You're going to be the skipper.'

Exasperation dimmed her elation. 'George . . .'

'Now, lass, you wouldn't want me to break my oath, solemnly made over two bottles of whisky, that I'd never work as a skipper again. I'll be there for you, just as I promised. Have I ever broken a promise?'

She was beaten and he knew it, but at least he would be there and that was the main thing. 'It's a deal. But no more drinking tonight. You've got to be stone-cold sober in the morning.'

'What a terrible thought!' He gave a mournful shake of the head and sighed.

'George . . .' she threatened.

He chuckled, his eyes merrily teasing her. 'Go on with you, Jilly. A man's got to do what a man's got to do. I can still see marlin a hundred foot under water and a mile away. It's the whisky that does it. Don't you worry about the morning. I'll be sharper-eyed than ever.'

She rolled her eyes at him, then gave him an affectionate hug before taking herself out of the busy bar. She felt great, right on top of the world which had looked so terribly grim since her father's accident. But it wasn't grim any more. It was shining with all sorts of wonderful possibilities.

And she was hungry, not having eaten anything since the gargantuan meal at Tawney's. She had been too uptight to swallow any food today, but now her stomach was nicely settled. Very nicely settled. She drove home, cooked and ate a satisfying meal, then telephoned Pamela.

'Jillian!' her friend squeaked. 'Did you get raped last night?'

Jillian winced. She didn't want to talk about last night. She didn't even want to think about last night. 'No, I didn't get raped,' she said dismissively.

But Pamela's avid curiosity was not willing to be dismissed. 'Lord! I've been worrying about you all day. How did it go?'

'Everything's been sorted out,' Jillian said very firmly. 'He's accepted the charter so, hopefully, I won't get back to the boutique until the season ends. You'd better hire a girl, Pamela. And you can take the accounts to Dad. He'll do them.'

'Will do. But what happened last night? Did his eyes fall out or did you chop his hands off?'

'I . . . er . . . used evasive tactics. You won't tell Dad about that dress, will you, Pamela?' she added anxiously.

'Mum's the word. But I still don't know how you got away with it. Tell me what happened!'

A rush of guilt and hot shame turned her mouth dry. She swallowed. 'We . . . we reached an understanding. I've got to go now. Talk to Dad if there's any problems with the boutique.'

'OK. But I'd like to hear about that understanding some time. I wish you the best of luck, Jillian.'

'Thanks. You, too.'

Jillian's cheeks were burning as she put the telephone down, but she hadn't really told a lie. Taylor had told her to forget it and she very much wanted to, so they did have an understanding of sorts. Her foolish behaviour had probably lost his respect for her as a woman, but at least now he respected her as a skipper, and overall he no longer had such a bad opinion of her. She remembered his smile and was encouraged. And he hadn't avoided her company today either.

The next morning Jillian dithered over what to wear. She wanted to look attractive but she didn't want Taylor Marshall getting wrong ideas about her again. She finally settled on her normal boat-gear:

blue deck-shoes, white shorts, and the 'Dreamcat-cher' T-shirt, with a sports bra under it. She twisted her long, blonde hair into a plait at the back of her head, hesitated over make-up, then decided against it. She never wore make-up on fishing trips and she didn't want old George commenting on it. Or teasing her once he saw Taylor Marshall. His shrewd old eyes would undoubtedly see soon enough that she was attracted to the big American but she didn't want to advertise it.

Jillian re-checked the clothes she had packed, nervously wondering if the dresses were all right. But if Taylor asked her to dine with him on the mother-ship . . . And he might—it was the usual practice for the charter to ask the skipper sometimes . . . and it wasn't as if the dresses were really sexy, just well-fitting and pretty. Her heart fluttered as she left them packed and zipped the bag shut again. She had to get going. She locked up the house and drove in to Cairns, imagining Taylor still in his bed and hoping he was dreaming dreams of her.

Old George was already on the boat, dead-set sober and all primed to tease her for her tardiness. Jillian was so pleased to see him that his good-natured joshing just rolled off her shoulders. Bob seemed even more cheerful than usual, and the three of them did all the chores so quickly that at half-past six they sat down to a cup of coffee. They were still in the cabin when Taylor Marshall surprised them, presenting himself on board ten minutes early, followed a little more apprehensively by Jerry Somers. Jillian smiled to herself as they showed their surprise at seeing old George. She performed the introductions and positively enjoyed the reactions when George took over.

'Up you go and get started, Jilly. These fellas are obviously keen for action. Reckon we'll take them out to Number Five Ribbon Reef.'

'Number Five? You said Seven yesterday, George,' she reminded him.

'And that's where all the boats went,' he answered smugly. 'But we're going to steal a march on them today. Number Five it is, lass. Take my word for it.'

'Whatever you say, George,' she assured him with a happy grin, and shot up the ladder to the fly-bridge.

She was still inwardly laughing at the look that had been on Taylor's face when he joined her for the trip up the channel. It sparkled in her eyes as she turned to him and bubbled, 'Lovely day, isn't it?'

'So you gave the old reprobate a job,' he said in an amused tone.

'He insisted on being the deckie,' she said solemnly, but her expressive blue eyes gave the laughter away.

Taylor lifted a quizzical eyebrow. 'He insisted?'

'Yes. I wanted him to be skipper.'

'Skipper?' Taylor echoed, completely nonplussed.

The laughter burst into an uninhibited peal of merriment. 'Oh, Taylor! He might look like an old reprobate but old George knows more about catching marlin than any skipper in the fleet. He had the lead boat for years before he retired and he taught Dad all he knows. There's no one better than George, and I only managed to prise him out of retirement because of a promise he made me.' She slanted him a dry look. 'You really shouldn't judge on appearances. Particularly in a place like Cairns.'

'So I see. Apparently I've been wrong twice already,' he said a little wryly. 'Very challenging place, Cairns. It's full of surprises.'

The reassessing look in his eyes sent a shiver of hope and dismay up Jillian's spine. Was he referring to the two meetings with George or was he thinking of the wattle-dress which had misled him about her, or the marlin that had got away? If it was the latter, then maybe she could get their relationship on to a more natural basis. And he had chosen to come up and talk to her instead of staying below with the other men. Surely that meant something.

Most of Taylor's conversation was impersonal, revolving around Cairns and big-game fishing. Jillian was dying to ask him personal questions about his life, but he didn't offer any information and she didn't dare to probe too closely. It was not a skipper's place to pry into the private business of a charter, and she didn't want to put any more feet wrong.

They reached Number Five Ribbon Reef all too soon for Jillian's liking. Old George called Taylor down even before she put the boat into a trolling pattern and she watched him descend the ladder with mixed feelings, seeing the eager light of anticipation in his eyes and wishing she could light the same expression.

'There's marlin here all right,' old George declared with relish. 'I can smell 'em.'

No sooner were they in deep water than a marlin hit the bait and the line screamed out. Everyone leapt to action stations, Taylor into the fighting-chair, Jerry Somers aiming his camera, George and Bob yelling instructions and Jillian manoeuvring the boat. Excitement rode high as the fish climbed out of the water.

'She's a good one!' Bob crowed. 'About six hundred pounds, eh George?'

'About that. Big enough to give you a good fight, me lad,' George tossed at Taylor who was working hard at pumping the rod.

It took him an hour to bring the marlin alongside, and George automatically tagged and released it. 'Why did you do that?' Taylor demanded. 'I just caught that fish!'

'And what would you be doing with it, a baby like that?' George retorted with a chortle. 'The other anglers would laugh you off the mother-ship if you towed that one in to be weighed. We always tag and release marlin under a thousand pounds. You're here for the game fishing, aren't you? Well, you've had your sport. No need to kill.'

George wasn't being entirely truthful, but Jillian had too much sympathy with his sentiments to correct him. The charter was entitled to make the choice of release or kill, but no skipper in Cairns ever recommended a kill. Game fishing on The Great Barrier Reef was an honour-sport, and catches were recorded on the skipper's word. The only exception to that was if the marlin looked to be a world record catch. Then it had to be officially weighed for IGFA recognition.

'What do you mean, tag?' asked Taylor in puzzlement.

George showed him the little dart which was jabbed into the marlin's side. 'See this little number here. We record that number along with the size of the marlin and where it was caught. The marine scientists know very little about marlin and they're trying to find out something about their migratory habits. If a tagged marlin is re-caught, then they learn something. Some we've tagged here have been caught off New Zealand and as far away as Peru. Fascinating study.'

Taylor nodded in agreement and Jillian sighed in relief. He wasn't a killer! She felt ridiculously proud of him, and her opinion of him rose even higher as the day wore on. He generously persuaded Jerry Somers to try his hand in the fighting-chair, and although the cameraman protested he was supposed to be taking videos, Taylor insisted that it was an experience he couldn't miss. Jerry lost one fish but caught two, much to his delight. Taylor himself caught four, and every catch was tagged and released. George had been right about Number Five Ribbon and it was an exhilarating day of fishing for everyone.

'Is it always like this?' Taylor asked incredulously as he joined Jillian for the short trip to the mother-ship.

She laughed and shook her head. 'I'm afraid not. Some days you won't even see marlin. Other days you'll see every other boat catching them but yours. It can be boring and frustrating. There's so much luck in the game, but with George on board, we've got a very big slice of it on our side.'

'You can say that again,' Taylor enthused. 'Some of the stories he was telling us were amazing!'

Jillian grinned at him and he laughingly threw up his hands. 'OK, I've been proved wrong. He's a great old guy. I love him. Satisfied?'

If only he would say that about her, Jillian thought,

and the thought made her heart lurch. Love? Had she fallen in love with Taylor Marshall? Was that this overwhelming feeling she had for him? Was it possible to fall in love with someone you hardly knew anything about? Someone you'd only known for a few days?

Jillian remembered the impact he had made on her when he had walked through the door at the airport terminal, but surely that was only the impact a very handsome man would make on any woman. Love at first sight was a myth, wasn't it? Love meant a great deal more than physical attraction. Was it his sexual appeal that coloured her perspective, causing her to look for and find other qualities that justified her response to him?

She threw a quick surreptitious glance at him, expecting his gaze to be drinking in the sea around them. It wasn't. It was fixed on her, drinking in the lissom length of her tanned legs and the curve of her bottom. Jillian instantly felt hot all over. She couldn't check the memory of him caressing her thighs, parting them, thrusting his own powerfully muscled leg between them. Was he remembering that?

'Tell me about this mother-ship, the *Eurydice*.'

Jillian almost jumped as Taylor spoke. His innocuous words shamed her. She had actually wanted him to be thinking of making love to her, and disappointment bit across her tumultuous thoughts.

'Does it live up to the way it was described in the brochures?' Taylor added, his tone one of casual interest.

Another impersonal question! Jillian mentally kicked herself. Even if Taylor did find her physically attractive to look at, he would also remember the metaphoric kick in the groin she had delivered. He wasn't going to give her another chance. What man would? She gritted her teeth against a sickening wave of despair and answered him.

'I don't know what degree of luxury you're used to, Taylor, but the *Eurydice* is the top-line accommodation for the fishing season here. It has twenty guest cabins, large entertainment areas and every possible facility that you can put on a boat. I believe it's generally chartered for conferences or private parties out of Brisbane or Surfers' Paradise the rest of the year. It's huge. 'We call it the Big Cat up here.'

He was still looking at her. She could feel his gaze concentrated on her, but whether it was on her body or her face she dared not check. Her nipples had hardened into taut buds and she felt far too self-conscious of the fact to turn towards him in any way.

Why the Big Cat?' he drawled, after a long pause which had increased Jillian's physical confusion.

She had to get her mind off him. He didn't care about her. It took a moment before she was confident of keeping her voice steady. Even then she could not trust herself to look at him as she spoke. 'Because of its twin hulls, like a catamaran, but of course the *Eurydice* isn't a sailing boat. The twin hulls give it the extra width for really spacious living. And stability.' Somehow she summoned up a dry smile and threw it at him. 'You won't even know you're on a boat tonight unless you walk out on deck.'

He had met her eyes with an intent, considering look which had seemed very personal. Jillian was thrown into confusion again.

'Are the decks spacious, too?'

She nodded, her mouth too dry to speak. Taylor stood up and very casually, as if to hold himself steady, put one hand on her shoulder. Jillian's pulse leapt into overdrive and the flesh under his hand grew disconcertingly warm. Her whole body tingled from his closeness. She could feel his warm breath on her ear.

'Have dinner with me tonight?' he murmured.

Had she imagined those words? Had she? Were they the product of all her feverish wishing? She darted an agitated glance at him, hoping, wanting, willing the words to have come from his lips. The melting brown eyes seemed to be waiting, expecting an answer. A lump of chaotic emotion blocked her throat.

'Jilly, you're supposed to be steering twenty-five degrees and I reckon we're doing about three hundred and twenty-five,' old George called up from the cockpit. 'Not that it matters if you want to eat dinner at Mount Isa or on top of a reef, but I don't reckon we'll make the mother-ship on this course.'

In dumb confusion, Jillian wrenched her eyes away from Taylor's and focussed them on the compass. Old George was right. With a guilty jerk she spun the wheel, correcting the bearing.

'That's better, lass,' said George drily.

Taylor sat down again, observing her intently as Jillian seethed with a multitude of conflicting emotions. He had asked her to dinner. All she had to do was say yes, just turn to him and say yes, thank you, I'd like that very much. So why was she acting like a gauche, tongue-tied teenager? It was ridiculous! And yet, the memory of that other dinner she had shared with him was cramping her natural instincts with a writhing mass of inhibitions.

'Isn't it the done thing for a charter to ask his skipper aboard the mother-ship for dinner?' Taylor asked quietly.

Her cheeks burned with self-conscious embarrassment. 'You can invite the whole crew if you like. It's . . .'

'Good idea!' And before Jillian could say another word, Taylor was leaning over the railing of the fly-bridge, shouting to the others. 'George . . . Bob . . . I want you all to come over to the mother-ship and have dinner with me tonight. I reckon we ought to celebrate today's catch. How about it?'

'I'll be in on that,' Bob answered eagerly. 'Thanks, Taylor.'

'Not for me, lad,' old George demurred. 'I'm for my bunk tonight. Haven't had so much exercise for quite some time and I've got to be ready for you tomorrow.'

'Whatever you say, George,' Taylor agreed good-naturedly. 'Bob and Jillian can make up for you.' His gaze swung back to her, confidently assuming her compliance. 'OK?'

He couldn't be thinking of sex if he was prepared to invite Bob and George to dinner too. Jillian was only too happy to nod. He smiled, and it was the smile of a man who had got his own way. Jillian's heart fluttered nervously. What did he want with her? What did he really want? Was he interested in her or did he simply want to celebrate with the people who had shared his exciting day?

She was still tormenting herself with that question an hour and a half later as she put the finishing touches to her make-up. Her hair was a wavy cloud around her shoulders. She had changed her dress twice, finally settling on the blue cotton-knit. The cross-over bodice was demurely frilled, and although the bow at the waist drew attention to the opening in the circular skirt, Jillian knew that the skirt overlap was deep enough to prevent any show of leg. It was a comfortable dress, feminine, and not really sexy except in so far as it hugged her curvaceous figure. But after all, Taylor had seen more of her figure in the shorts and T-shirt she had worn all day.

Old George was sitting over a tot of whisky when she emerged from her cabin and he shook his head knowingly as he took in her appearance. 'That's a pretty big piece of Oklahoma you're eating with tonight, Jilly. I hope you're not fishing in dangerous waters.'

She sighed and slanted him a wry smile. 'I hope so, too, George. Did Taylor say he'd come from Oklahoma or is that a shrewd guess on your part?'

'He said that's where he hails from. And that's where he'll be returning to in twelve days' time. Don't be forgetting that, Jilly,' he added warningly. 'I wouldn't like to see you hurt, lass.,

Jillian knew that was probably inevitable now. She was already too emotionally involved with Taylor Marshall to shrug him off lightly, and the twelve days deadline was all too sharply imbedded in her mind to forget it. Twelve days . . . and nights, her heart urged. She put on a carefree face. 'I don't want to see you hurt either, George, so go easy on the whisky before you roll into your bunk.'

'Cheeky!' George tossed after her, but Jillian's thoughts were already leaping ahead. Taylor was waiting for her. She would be having dinner with him. And then?

Bob grinned at her as she climbed into the dinghy he was holding steady against the boat. 'Taylor's a good bloke, isn't he?' From Bob it was the top accolade.

'I like him,' Jillian returned blithely, and knew she was speaking only half the truth. She turned her gaze to the *Eurydice* and hoped quite fiercely that Taylor was not just a big cat on the prowl for a temporary meal.

CHAPTER FIVE

To Jillian's eyes, the *Eurydice* didn't even look like a boat. Its two-storey superstructure dominated its lines, proclaiming the craft's purpose: accommodation and entertainment plus, with privacy guaranteed by the sea. Jillian had heard that the boat was frequently used as a floating casino, and she didn't doubt the story. Anything went on the water, and it was not at all uncommon to see the wives and girlfriends of anglers sunbathing nude while their men fished.

Taylor was not looking out for her arrival. Jillian scanned the decks of the *Euridyce* without being able to pick him out. There was a gathering of people on the large aft-deck, watching the weigh-in of the marlin which had been towed to the mother-ship by other fishing boats. The gantry which hung between the twin hulls was always the main focus of interest at this time of day, much more so to anglers than the brilliant panorama of the setting sun, Jillian thought sourly. She had never understood the attraction of dead marlin and never would. It turned her stomach to see such magnificent creatures of the sea hauled out of their natural habitat and hung up for the supposed triumph of man.

It surprised Jillian when she stepped on board that Taylor was at hand to greet her. It did not seem to matter what he wore, he looked fantastic. The open-necked maroon shirt and light fawn slacks lent a casual elegance to his muscular frame and emphasised his dark colouring, somehow making his very masculine beauty even more striking. His smile showed off the white perfection of his teeth and the brown eyes sparkled appreciation as they swept Jillian from head to foot and back up to meet her rather wary gaze.

'Wow again!' he said softly.

Her heart did a double-loop. Taylor's reaction to her appearance was too uncomfortably close to that made over the wattle-dress. She wanted to correct any false impression he might still have of her but there was no opportunity. Bob was just behind her and Earl Schultz was at Taylor's shoulder, already holding out his hand in a show of peace-making.

'Hope you'll accept my apology for underestimating you, Miss Howard,' he said with every appearance of sincerity and even a dash of charm. 'Taylor's been singing your praises about today's fishing and I sure was impressed by yesterday's performance.'

Jillian found her tongue with some difficulty. 'Thank you, Mr Schultz. How is Gordon?'

'He'll be fine. Luckily there was no permanent damage done. I saw your father, too and he very generously offered to give Gordon a bit of company while they were both in hospital.' His mouth curled into a self-deprecating smile. 'Fine man, your father. Guess I was a bit too quick at shooting off my mouth the other day.'

'Perfectly understandable,' Jillian demurred quickly, grateful that everything had been smoothed over.

Earl Schultz offered his hand to Bob. 'And my appreciation to you, too, Bob. Never seen a man more on his toes, except perhaps Taylor here, when he's on a football field.'

'A bit slow at other times,' Taylor muttered with a grin at Jillian which curled her toes.

He was thinking of the other night! And his arm curved possessively around her waist as he drew her with him towards the aft-deck. Had he forgiven her for that dreadful fiasco? He was acting as if everything was fine between them, so fine that he could make a joke about the frustration she had given him. And he was very definitely attracted to her. That look in his eyes ... the hand resting lightly on her waist ... A very pleasurable warmth tingled around her veins. Taylor really must like her.

'There were a couple of big catches on other boats today,' he remarked as they strolled on to the aft-deck. He waved towards the gantry where two huge marlin were hanging by their tails. 'They really are an awesome size.'

'Yes,' Jillian bit out and when he would have drawn her forward for a closer look, she jerked out of his hold, shuddering with distaste. She averted her gaze, staring out at the dying rays of the sun. Bob and Earl walked past, their attention riveted on the fish. Taylor stayed with her but she was conscious of his frowning puzzlement. His hand ran lightly down her arm and she shuddered again at the deliberate caress. But not from distaste.

'You couldn't be cold, Jillian. Is it me ... or the fish?' he asked quietly.

She flashed him an apologetic look. 'I know it's

silly, but I hate seeing them dead. They're so beautiful alive ... strong and fast, courageous and powerful.'

His frown smoothed out and he took her hand, separating her fingers with his and gripping with a strength which made her feel oddly fragile. His eyes probed hers with unnerving intensity. 'I hope you'll think of me like that some day,' he murmured.

Jillian's heart performed a crazy jiggle. Was he suggesting there could be some future to their relationship? 'I ... I already do,' she stammered, wanting him to say more.

He smiled and a mischievous twinkle broke the intensity which had held her mesmerised. 'Now I understand old George's subtle pressure to tag and release. He was looking after your sensibilities.'

'No!' Jillian denied swiftly. 'Ask any skipper. It's the general policy to tag and release. All the giant marlin are female, you know. No one's caught a male marlin bigger than about three hundred pounds. For three months every year the giant marlin come here to spawn. The Great Barrier Reef is their breeding ground. A marlin like that...' she nodded towards the gantry, '... carries literally millions of eggs. Tens of millions,' she added with all the passion of a conservationist.

'So you're trying to protect the game fishing industry,' Taylor commented cynically.

She sighed, disappointed by his attitude. 'No. The few that anglers catch are barely a fraction of the thousands that the Japanese long-line fishermen hook on just one fifty-mile line. I don't like seeing them dead, but that's a personal feeling which has nothing to do with my job as skipper. You're entitled to do what you want with any fish you catch. Make your own choice,' she added flatly.

For what seemed terribly long moments Taylor observed her bright eyes and heightened colour with a sphinx-like expression which gave her no inkling of his thoughts. Then he smiled. 'I think I've already made it. Let's go into the saloon. I'll get you a drink.'

Jillian was helpless against that smile, even more helpless at controlling her reaction to his touch as he took her elbow and steered her into the luxurious saloon. It had a club atmosphere with its thick, berber carpet and brown leather settees and an extremely well-stocked bar, on which several men were resting their elbows. Jillian wished she could be alone with Taylor, but any evening on a mother-ship was a very social occasion. As she sipped a pre-dinner sherry, several other skippers came up to congratulate her on the day's catch.

'I can see we'll have to get on the radio to you, Jilly, or follow your tail. How did you shanghai old George? And where is the canny devil?' her father's closest competitor for lead boat enquired, with a touch of chagrin.

Jillian laughed. 'He stayed on board, sharpening up his nose with a bottle of whisky.'

'And where does he reckon he'll smell out marlin tomorrow?'

'You'll have to follow our tail, Harvey.'

He shook his head in disgust. 'Lose Jack and get George. A man never gets a break.'

'I wouldn't underestimate Jillian either,' Taylor warned good-humouredly. 'She's quite a skipper.'

Jillian glowed under the praise even as Harvey grumbled, 'Jack's daughter! What can you expect? But tomorrow's another day, my girl.'

Taylor continued to compliment her throughout the conversation over dinner. Other anglers stopped by their table, envious that seven marlin had been hooked up by *Dreamcatcher*. Earl Schultz was almost bursting with anticipation which Bob cheerfully fed with fishing stories. It was a very convivial meal, enjoyed in a party atmosphere.

The modern décor provided classy but casual comfort. Directors' chairs in chrome and tan leather were easily moved from table to table and, since the *Eurydice* was here for the season, the walls of the dining-room were festooned with photographs of marlin and anglers in contest with one another, which inevitably incited a swapping of experiences amongst the guests.

Taylor sat opposite Jillian, and, even while she laughed and chatted with others, never once was she unaware of his almost constant gaze on her. She was more than flattered by his fixed interest. She was thrilled out of her mind, and far too excited to do justice to the four-course meal which was served. As she waved away the sweets, Taylor raised a teasingly quizzical eyebrow.

'Not so hungry tonight?'

She flushed at the all-too-pertinent observation and subsequently stammered, 'Er ... no. No, I'm not.' More than ever she wanted to explain her idiotic behaviour on their first night together.

Taylor pushed back his chair and stood up, his eyes twinkling devilment. 'Then I suggest a stroll around

the deck. It'll stimulate your appetite for tomorrow,'
he said cheerfully.

Jillian's flush grew hotter but she wanted to be
alone with him, if for nothing else but to set him
straight. She stood up and they excused themselves
from the company. As soon as Taylor's arm went
around her waist for the walk out of the room, Jillian
knew she wanted much more than a clarifying
conversation. She wanted him to hold her close and
kiss her as he had kissed her on their way to Tawney's.
And mean it with all his heart.

Taylor led her to the fore-deck, which was
completely deserted since the rest of the guests were
still lingering over their meal. She turned to him
quickly, wanting all explanations out of the way. 'I
hope ... um ... I hope you're not thinking this is the
same as ... er ... the other night.'

'Certainly not,' he stated emphatically and steered
her over to the railing. 'I don't think about that at all,'
he assured her, then smiled a lazy, slow smile. 'But
you can't blame me for my dreams.'

Excitement pumped her heart faster. Had Taylor
been dreaming about her, as she had been dreaming
about him? Every good intention of stating her case
was smashed into nothingness as he gently pulled her
into a loose embrace. His hands locked behind her
waist, imprisoning her in his own private world as he
moved the lower part of her body towards his own.

There was a full moon, shedding its pale glitter on
the ever-rippling ocean, creating as romantic a scene
as any would-be lover might wish, but Jillian had no
eyes for it. The man holding her was totally
dominant. She leaned back against his arms, her

hands lightly resting on his chest, feeling the warmth of his body through the thin shirt. She wanted to move her hands upwards to the opening where his bare throat glistened invitingly, so strong, so ... manly, but she found the strength of that desire rather alarming. Her gaze fluttered up to his face, hoping to find in his expression the same burning urgency and need which she felt.

Even though the distinctive planes of his features were clearly delineated in the soft moonlight, Jillian could read nothing from them. The deep-set eyes were shadowed by the aggressive cast of his brow, yet she sensed rather than saw an intense aliveness flashing in their depths, a sharper awareness than she had ever felt from Taylor before.

The cool sea-breeze feathered tendrils of hair around her face and fanned a latent sensuality which wanted to be fed. The sound of waves lapping the twin hulls seemed to reinforce the beating of her heart. Surely if it got any louder Taylor must hear it!

He gathered her closer, pressing her more intimately against him. Jillian closed her eyes, sure that they could not help revealing her love and need for him. A sigh of brimming emotion parted her lips. How was it possible to feel so much a captive of a man who was exerting no force over her?

His lips brushed over hers, lightly, undemandingly, teasingly, again and again, slowly gathering more intense nuances of pressure. With one arm he held her pinned to him while his other hand found erotic spots down her spine that totally mesmerised Jillian. She shivered ecstatically in his embrace and the hand glided upwards, under the soft curtain of her hair, to ignite an exquisite sensitivity around the nape of her neck. A moan of pleasure whispered from her throat, and as if he had been waiting to capture it, his mouth covered hers with possessive fervour. His fingers slid through her hair, exerting an inexorable pressure which allowed no escape as he deepened the kiss, his tongue sliding between her lips, seeking, demanding admission.

Her hands scrabbled up his chest, clutching at his shoulders, then sliding of their own volition around his neck, bringing her into full body contact with him. His warmth seeped through the flimsy cotton of her summer dress, swelling into her breasts, making them tingle with an excitement that hardened her nipples and sent nervous little thrills through her body, thrills that became more electric as he thrust her closer, moulding her softness to an instant knowledge of his arousal. She gasped as a purely womanly weakness flooded through her, and in that same instant of dazing vulnerability, he invaded her mouth with an erotic penetration that carried unleashed passion.

This was no sensual exploration, but an act of possession, and for one split second, Jillian felt the quivering shock of absolute violation. Then a wild exultation was racing through her veins. She didn't think. She didn't want to think. Taylor wanted her, and she loved him, wanted to give him everything, to please him, to make him love her. She gave him all the love in her heart, responding with a surrender which was also a need to know his heart. In her own feverish passion was a searching of his desire, a plea that pulsed through every womanly movement of her soft body ... I want you to love me, Taylor. Just a little. Any bit will do. I'll give you anything you want if you'll love me.

As if he sensed her resolve, he crushed her lower body into even more intimate contact with his and she melted into his hardness. A hand tugged at the bow which held her dress together, loosened it, then swept around the edge of her bodice, pushing it down over her shoulders. Jillian didn't resist. She couldn't. His hand plucked the ripe fullness of her breast from its lacy half-bra, kneading the soft flesh with gentle fingers as his palm moved in an erotic rotation over her sensitised nipple.

She writhed with the pleasure of his touch and was shaking with her own vulnerability when Taylor withdrew from the kiss. He sucked in a sharp breath and a long sigh feathered against her sensitised lips, making her catch her own breath. She opened her eyes to the feverish glitter of his and was totally lost to the burning intensity of his desire. He wanted her. Surely he was feeling the same overwhelming emotion that possessed her.

With a wild, primitive growl he swung her over to the edge of the deck, spreading her legs apart with his own as he pressed her against the railing, thrusting his own urgency to her pliant womanhood. Again his mouth plundered hers and she wanted to give him ... needed to give him ... longed to give him everything he had ever wanted from a woman. Her hands crept under the open collar of his shirt, relishing the moist heat of his skin, delicately feeling for the sensitive pressure spots he had found on her, wanting to excite him further, pleasure him, love him.

He suddenly shuddered under her touch. His hand squeezed her breast in pleasure-pain. His mouth writhed on hers. He pressed his body more urgently, swaying in an erotic rhythm which was almost barbaric. Jillian knew instinctively that he was losing all control and she exulted in the fact. He was hers. He had to love her and she was dying for him to take her.

Then suddenly the pressure on her bruised but exquisitely tender mouth eased to a softness that she sensed was a withdrawal. Jillian tried to hold the kiss, wanting to cling on to the memory which she would always hold dear, a moment in time she would never forget, but she could not regain the searing intensity. Taylor was fighting to control his passions, but he rubbed his lips lightly over hers, and his heavy breathing against those sensitised surfaces was unbelievably exciting. She did not want it to end. She did not care what happened. She wanted to give herself to this man. She loved him.

She gave a little cry of protest as his mouth left hers, but the cry changed into a whimper of exquisite torment when his head bent to her exposed breast and his tongue swept over her erect nipple, lashing it back and forth. Then he took it and the surrounding areola in his mouth and gently sucked at her until Jillian almost fainted with the melting ecstasy which was turning her limbs to quivering jelly. She was bereft of all her senses, totally open to him, exposed to him, existing only for him to take.

He lifted his head and straightened up, pulling her with him. She opened her eyes, total surrender swimming in them as she looked into his. His face was turned to the moonlight now, and it seemed odd to her that it held an inscrutable expression. His eyes seemed sharp, more coldly calculating than hot with passion. His mouth curved a little and shaped words.

'First down.'

The soft murmur was barely audible to her ears but the sound floated into her mind and struck a discordant note. His mouth swooped on hers again, seeking out the promise she had been giving him. He plundered all its sweetness with an insistence which was no longer concerned with persuading a response.

The words he had spoken niggled at Jillian's dazed mind, searching for some relevant meaning. They connected to a vague memory with a jolt. No, he couldn't mean that, her own need argued, wanting the excitement to continue, but already it was wavering with uncertainty. She pushed Taylor's head back, her eyes focusing on his with growing urgency. She hesitated to ask but she had to know.

'Doesn't that mean . . .' She could hardly recognise her own voice. It was furry with a terrible mixture of emotions. 'In your kind of football, doesn't that mean that you've made ten yards, and you win the chance to play for more ground?'

'That's right, honey,' he breathed with rich satisfaction. 'You get to play again.' And the kiss he gave her held all the rampaging thrust of a man certain of victory.

The passion which had been running riot in Jillian's veins was quenched by a wave of disillusionment. He didn't love her. Not even a little bit. She had stopped him in his tracks that first night, unwittingly throwing him a sexual challenge which he had obviously decided to take up . . . to play again! As much as she wanted to cling on to him, she knew she would only be fooling herself, hurting herself, because he didn't really want what she wanted to give. Unless she was mistaken. Maybe she was reading him wrongly, hope whispered. Maybe it was just his way of talking. She pushed some distance between them again.

Before she could speak, he took the initiative. 'You're right. We have to move from here,' he breathed raggedly, and pulled her bra-strap and dress back into place. 'We'll go down to my cabin and . . .'

'Wait a minute!' Jillian panted in mounting panic. Her hands scrambled to straighten her dress and tie the bow securely, ashamed of her wantonness and needing the protection of clothes against what he could do to her. 'I . . . I want to know what you meant by that? The . . . the first down?'

He gave a low, throaty chuckle which sent a shiver down her spine. His hands spanned her waist and her legs turned to water as she waited for his answer. His eyes seemed to flash with triumph as the chuckle faded into a wholly sensual smile.

'A first down is the initial drive towards a touchdown, the end goal, so to speak, and it's a touchdown I want with you, honey-girl. Or to put it another way . . .' He paused and the smile turned into a grin. 'The other night you said you were the one that got away. Well, if I'm reading your response right, I don't think you'll last out the charter.'

Jillian wanted to die. Right there on the spot. She had thought him kind and considerate and sensitive. He wasn't. He was hard and callous and vain. All he cared about was getting his own way with her, all on his terms. It stunned her that she had been so wrong about him. Tension screamed through her body as he would have pulled her close again. He frowned at her stiffness and grabbed hold of her hips when she tried to step away.

'Isn't this what you want?' he rasped, finally taking in the frozen horror on her face.

All the melting softness inside her had congealed into a sour lump that curdled her stomach. Even her tongue tasted bitter as she spat out her answer. 'If that's what you want, Taylor Marshall, just pass a discreet word to the skipper of the *Eurydice*. He'll contact the call-girl service in Cairns. I understand that girls are frequently flown out to mother-ships and I'm sure you'll be able to get any service you wish.'

The affront stamped on his face only fuelled her bitterness. 'I regret that my reckless choice of dress the other night misled you into thinking I was ready, willing and able to serve your convenience while you're here, because nothing could be further from the truth.'

'My convenience!' His fingers dug into her flesh and his face was black with suffused rage. 'If I was inclined towards convenience' ... he sneered the word ... 'I would have ordered it before I got here.'

'Well, you're not ordering me into your bed, or leading me there either,' Jillian retorted fiercely. 'If I wanted that it'd be on my terms, not yours!'

'Your terms! You're nothing but a vicious little tease!'

Jillian went ice-cold. She supposed it did look that way to him, but it wasn't so and her own self-esteem demanded a correction. 'You're wrong! So wrong . . .

He laughed in her face, a bitter, contemptuous laugh. 'Then with your acting ability, Jilly' . . . he made the affectionate diminutive an acid derision of any suggestion of innocence . . . 'you ought to be in movies, not me. You'd be the hottest box-office of the decade.'

'No, I couldn't match you, Taylor,' she shot at him miserably, then punched his hands away and turned her back on him. Her legs were trembling so much that her first step was a lurch, and Taylor grasped her shoulders and spun her around before she recovered her balance.

'If I wanted a call-girl . . .' His voice held blistering outrage. 'God damn it! I've never been with a whore in my life!'

No, he wouldn't have ever found that necessary, not when he could probably snap his fingers for a girl, Jillian thought bitterly. He had only persisted with her because she had got away the first time. She gritted her teeth. 'You let me go, Taylor Marshall, or I'll scream my lungs out, and I figure there are a few gentlemen around who will come to my aid.'

He picked his hands off her with an air of utter contempt. 'Yes, and you'd suck them right in, as you did me, wouldn't you?'

The stinging accusation brought tears to her eyes. Even now, when she knew him to have no real feeling for her, she still couldn't bear his condemnation. She lifted her chin in wounded pride. 'Have you ever felt desperate, Taylor? Desperate enough to try anything to safeguard the future of someone you love? My father was going to lose his boat if you didn't take the charter. So I was crazy enough to think I could ... I could hold on to you by ... by wearing that dress, but ...' She shook her head, too distressed to go on. 'I'm sorry,' she choked out.

'There's no question about the charter tonight,' Taylor jeered at her.

'No,' she agreed, 'there isn't. But I'm a fool in more ways than one, and I ... I'm inexperienced with men. I can't match up to you,' she confessed miserably, and fled, almost stumbling in her haste to get away from him.

Taylor did not follow her. Jillian plunged into a wash-room and stayed there until she could compose herself enough to face other people. She felt totally wretched and drained of all energy. It took all her pride and will-power to smooth over the ragged ends of her nerves and assume a façade of unruffled dignity. She was very much afraid that if she saw Taylor again the façade would collapse in an ignoble heap, but she steeled herself to enter the dining-room.

Bob was still chatting with Earl Schultz and Jerry Somers over the table. Taylor was still absent. Jillian hurried to the table, tapped Bob on the shoulder and spoke with a command that privately amazed her. 'I want to go now, Bob. Are you ready?'

'Sure,' he agreed good-naturedly.

She quickly bade goodnight to Earl and Jerry, told them they would be picked up at nine-thirty in the morning, and left before any enquiry was made as to Taylor's whereabouts. Luckily Bob did not see anything amiss in her behaviour and he chatted about the Americans as he puttered the dinghy back to *Dreamcatcher*.

Jillian was intensely relieved to shut herself in her own little cabin where she could give in to her misery. Long into the night she thought about Taylor, and her heart grew heavier and heavier. Everything she had done with him had turned out badly, starting from the very beginning with her challenge about catching a world record marlin. Pricking a male ego was very dangerous and it had back-fired on her with a vengeance, and it was no use fooling herself that she hadn't meant to challenge him.

She had wanted his interest, but apparently Taylor Marshall only had one kind of interest in girls, and that was strictly below the belt. Her own sense of humiliation made her fiercely glad that she had frustrated his purpose and got away again. And she would stay away, Jillian determined, ignoring the pain in her heart. Impossible to catch her dream, she concluded in the blackest of despairs.

CHAPTER SIX

JILLIAN made sure she was already on the fly-bridge with the motors running when the American party came aboard the next morning. She called out a general greeting without even looking at Taylor. Luckily her Polaroid glasses, which were so necessary for spotting fish in the sunlit waters, also hid a multitude of sins, and she was very grateful for their usefulness in this situation. As soon as the dinghy was safely stowed away she steered straight for the fishing grounds that old George had designated.

Taylor did not join her on the fly-bridge for the trip. Jillian did not expect him to or want him to. She did not want to see, speak to, or even think about Taylor Marshall; he had already been the focus of far too many thoughts, most of them extremely painful. She concentrated hard on blocking him out. It was a fine day, a beautiful blue-skied day, and the water sparkled like crystal. It was too good a day to be spoilt by brooding over a man, especially an egomaniac like Taylor Marshall who didn't care whom he trampled or how he trampled over them, as long as he won. He certainly wasn't worth the persistent ache in her heart.

And Jillian's sour opinion of him was confirmed later in the day when Earl Schultz finally hauled in a nine hundred pound marlin. 'Tag and release?' old

George suggested matter-of-factly. 'Hell, no! That's the biggest damned fish I've ever caught. I want a photograph of me beside it,' Earl declared. And Taylor Marshall stood by and said not a word. No argument from him. He didn't give a damn for anyone or anything but himself.

Bob and old George gaffed the fish and hauled it into the cockpit through the transom door, while Jerry Somers skipped out of the way in nervous haste. Earl Schultz's face was alight with triumph. Taylor stared down at the fish for a long time as the iridescent blue faded into the dull black colour of death, then he turned away and gazed out to sea.

'That'll do me for the day!' Earl crowed. 'What do you say, Taylor? Want to stay out any longer or will we head back to the mother-ship?'

'Suits me,' he tossed over his shoulder carelessly.

Jillian gunned the motors with savage pleasure. She wanted them and their fish off the boat as soon as possible. When they arrived back at their mooring near the mother-ship, it was all she could do to reply politely to Earl Schultz's happy accolades as to her handling of the boat during his fight with the marlin. Jillian wished she had botched the job.

There was no invitation to dinner. Not that she would have accepted but it was perfectly clear that Taylor Marshall no longer thought it was worth his while to offer hospitality. Bob took them over to the mother-ship, towing the marlin alongside the dinghy. Old George hosed down the cockpit again and then poured out two tots of whisky, handing one to Jillian with a sympathetic grimace.

'Win some, lose some,' he muttered.

'I guess so,' she sighed dispiritedly.

'Get that drink down you, lass. Looks to me as though you need it,' came the gentle advice.

Jillian took off her glasses and rubbed her eyes. They weren't the only part of her that felt strained, but she didn't think whisky was going to relax her. She didn't even like whisky. Old George settled on to the bench seat behind the table and eyed her with concern. Jillian sat at the end and toyed with the glass he had given her, too despondent to offer conversation.

He reached across the table and patted her hand. 'The path of true love never did run smooth, Jilly,' he said in sad sympathy.

So he knew, Jillian thought miserably. Of course the change in Taylor's behaviour towards her between yesterday and today had to have been obvious to everyone, but George's shrewd old eyes had seen deeper than that. She looked up wearily to find him observing her all too intently, all too knowingly.

'There's no problem, George. We've both sorted out precisely what we mean to each other,' she said truthfully.

'Ah . . .' He nodded a few times, his expression still troubled. 'That's good,' he finally declared. 'I thought you were falling in love with him, lass.'

Jillian's mouth tightened. 'I couldn't care less what happens to Taylor Marshall. In fact, I hope a giant marlin pulls him straight into the water and drowns him. I certainly wouldn't be leaping overboard to save him,' she added vehemently.

Too vehemently. Old George sighed and shook his head. 'There's plenty of fish left in the sea, Jilly. Even big ones,' he added softly.

She sighed and threw him a wry look. 'You never married, George.'

'No, I never did,' he replied even more softly. 'But that's another story. Maybe I wasn't good enough.'

The echo of old regret touched her heart. She reached across and squeezed his hand. 'I think you are, George. Good enough for anybody,' she defended stoutly.

His mouth settled into a grimly determined line. 'Don't you worry, lass. I'm here and one way or another I'll see that no harm comes to you.'

It comforted her to know how deeply old George cared about her. Just like her father. They would love her and stand by her no matter what she did. Her spirits lifted a little. Her Dad and old George were worth ten of Taylor Marshall! Somehow she would shut that damned American out of her heart.

But resolution was easy. Carrying it through was much more difficult. Taylor completely confounded Jillian the next day. Earl brought in another big marlin and Taylor ordered it tagged and released, then set about persuading Earl into a conservationist line of thought, and crowning his argument with the fact that Jerry's video of the catch was much better value than a still photograph anyway. After that, all the marlin they caught were tagged and released as a matter of course.

And so it continued, day after day. Taylor

continued to ignore Jillian, except for the occasional polite interchange, but the fish went free. Jillian found that she could not ignore Taylor. She pretended to, but she was always aware of him, aware of the friendly conversations he held with Bob and old George, aware of his generous consideration of Jerry Somers who was given at least one turn in the fighting-chair every day, aware that, despite Earl's superiority of years, the agent-manager had a very healthy respect for Taylor's opinion. Taylor Marshall was very likeable and everyone, even old George, automatically responded to him. Jillian grew more and more miserable.

It was the sixth day before they hooked up a really giant marlin and, as luck would have it, it was Taylor's turn in the chair. Excitement ran high.

'By God! It's as big as a whale!' Earl Schultz cried.

'She's a real big mother all right,' Bob declared in awed delight. 'What do you reckon, George?'

'Thirteen hundred pound for sure. She'll be testing you, me lad.' He grinned at Taylor, who was already strained to the limit, trying to reel any line in.

For three hours he fought the huge and wily fish, and Jillian was called upon to manoeuvre the boat with fast and fierce concentration. Even so, she was not fast enough when the marlin dived under the boat in an unexpected change of direction. The line broke. Taylor wearily lifted the rod back into its slot in the armrest and collapsed forward in an effort to relieve his overworked muscles. The others gathered around, patting his back in congratulations for a grand effort. He heaved himself stiffly from the chair, turned towards the fly-bridge, put his hands on his hips and arched his back.

Jillian could not tell if he was looking at her, and whether his eyes held reproach or accusation. He was wearing Polaroid sunglasses too. Even though she knew she had done her best, she felt guilty that the fish had got away. Because it had been Taylor's fish.

'I'm sorry, Taylor,' she called out self-consciously, then with a squirming feeling of failure added, 'If you'd like George to skipper you next time, I'm sure he'd oblige you.'

That spun old George around to stare up at her. 'You gone crazy, lass? You did a great job!' He jutted his raggedy beard aggressively at Taylor. 'Have you got any complaints, me lad?'

'Did I say a word, George?' he demanded good-humouredly.

'Nope. That you didn't,' George agreed, then muttered darkly, 'but I reckon there's a few you could say if you had a mind to.'

Jillian jerked around from the railing and fiddled with the controls, suffering a severe rush of blood to the head. Old George had no right to say anything to Taylor. Not about her! She had tried to hide her inner misery from George but it seemed she had been unsuccessful. She knew he only spoke out of his concern for her but such words could only cause awkwardness for Taylor and the worst kind of embarrassment for herself. She would get over Taylor Marshall. She really would. In time. But the pain in her heart was now worse than ever.

'Mind if I join you?'

The blood which had rushed to her head very promptly left it. She threw one agonised look at Taylor who was poised at the top of the ladder, then kept her gaze rigidly fixed on the water. 'It's your boat for the day. You can be wherever you wish,' she answered stiffly.

He subsided on to the bench seat. Jillian swallowed several times, trying to clear the ringing dizziness in her head and also moisten a throat which had gone very dry. Damn George! Damn, damn, damn, old George! The last thing she wanted was pity from Taylor! Or kindness! Or even consideration! His presence only served to remind her of what she didn't have from him.

'I don't think it was your fault that the fish got away, Jillian,' he said quietly. 'It was simply the better contestant on the day.'

Oh God! What could she say to that? Her mind was an absolute blank. And it was her fault in a way. A skipper of old George's experience, or her father's, would have read the next move correctly. They could even think like marlin. 'You wanted a giant marlin,' she muttered dispiritedly, wishing he would go while every instinct screamed a desire for him to stay with her. Stay with her for ever.

He heaved a sigh and spoke very softly, barely audible above the noise of the engines. 'A man can want a lot of things, but that doesn't mean he should have them, or take them. In my experience the best things are those you earn. I regret that I didn't remember that with you.'

Her heart catapulted around her chest. Did he

mean ... Could he mean that he wished he had handled their relationship differently? That he still wanted her? If there was any possible chance she had to speak. 'I ...' It was a croak. She swallowed again and forced out words which carried a shaky undertone of hope. 'I don't blame you for what you thought of me. It was my own fault. And I'm sorry that you ... that I ...' She floundered in a sea of nightmarish memories.

'No, dammit!' he cut in with swift vehemence. 'I should have recognised inexperience, Jillian, no matter what façade you put up. God knows I've been around long enough! Too damned long! I can't even see what's in front of me any more. But I'm looking now, and I like what I see. I have from the beginning. Is here any chance of your forgiving me for what I was?'

Relief flooded through her and she turned to him with a smile of pure happiness. 'I like you, too, Taylor. I guess ...' She blushed. 'I guess I made that pretty obvious to you.'

His face relaxed into a grin. 'Not by the way you kept running away from me,' he said lightly.

A confusion of emotion made her turn away and instantly he was on his feet beside her, a reassuring hand gently squeezing her shoulder. 'Hey ... I don't want to frighten you away again. I want us to be friends. Can we try that?'

Friends! When just a casual touch from him could reduce her insides to churning jelly? But anything was better than not being with him. 'Yes. Yes, of course,' she got out huskily.

'Then just to show you forgive me, will you have dinner with us tonight? I promise you I won't do anything you don't want yourself,' he pressed persuasively.

The whole problem was what she did want, but she could not deny herself the pleasure of his company, no matter how great was the risk of being hurt. 'All right,' she agreed in quick response, unable to keep a note of eagerness out of her voice. She darted a glance at him and wasn't sure if she saw relief or satisfaction in his eyes. But whatever it was it had been warm.

'I'll go and see if I can persuade old George to come too. Would you like that?'

Her laughter was full of bubbling joy. Taylor really was sincere in his intentions if he was happy to invite an eagle-eyed George to be with them. 'He may not come but you can try,' she smiled, her eyes dancing her pleasure at his generosity.

'I like getting my own way, or don't you know that?' he declared blithely and gave her a mischievous wink as he took to the ladder on his way down to George.

If only she could get her own way with him, Jillian thought hopefully. There were only eight days left. Eight days to make the most of Taylor's offer of friendship. Eight days in which to win his heart, if that was at all possible.

They were days which passed all too quickly for Jillian, blissfully happy days that Taylor shared with her in friendly companionship. There were times when Jillian ached to be held close to him, when she felt like begging him to kiss her, and gradually frustration frayed the edge of her happiness. The time left grew shorter and shorter. She yearned for him with a depth of intensity that was painful at times, but there seemed no solution to her problem. Taylor was the perfect gentleman with her, treating her with the utmost respect and courtesy and never attempting even the smallest sexual advance. He showed no frustration with the platonic state of their relationship. It was as if he had switched off all desire for her, and it became increasingly difficult for Jillian to hide her despair.

The third last day of fishing came and went, and on the way back to the mother-ship, Taylor's manner to Jillian was exactly the same cheerful friendliness of the previous days. A tense frustration crept into her responses as he chatted away, seemingly without a care in the world besides enjoying the moment. She was so wretchedly aware of every physical attraction he possessed that it was almost torture to look at him and Jillian gradually fell into a brooding silence.

'Something wrong?' Taylor asked in quizzical concern.

She flashed him a forced smile and found his eyes too sharply probing for her comfort. 'A bit tired, that's all,' she said quickly, trying to shrug off the pall around her heart.

'Oh!' It was the sound of disappointment. 'I was going to ask you if you'd come scuba-diving around the reef with me tonight. I did go down one morning a week ago and found it as fantastic as you'd promised. I thought I'd like to try a night dive but if you don't ...'

'No, I'd love to,' Jillian cut in, pouring enthusiasm into her voice. She was not going to miss one minute with Taylor, no matter what she felt. 'But we'll have to go easy on dinner if we're diving,' she warned.

His grin seemed to dance with satisfaction. 'I'll order some supper for afterwards.'

There was little satisfiction for Jillian. She managed to stifle her own desires over the dinner-table that night by talking non-stop about the wonders of the coral reefs, telling Taylor how they had been built up over thousands of years by the constant reproduction of the tiny coral polyps. He listened with avid interest as she told him the reef was like a high-density urban development. So many marine creatures lived on it that homes changed hands at sundown. The big-eyed night roamers—spiny squirrel-fish, dainty red cardinals—left their coral caves and the butterfly, angel and surgeon fish moved in, replete after a day's foraging.

She explained that the most spectacular difference in the reef between night and day was in the coral polyps. By day most species were withdrawn inside their cup-like limestone casings, but at night they extended their bodies and tentacles to eat and assume the delicate blossom-like appearance that for centuries had made naturalists assume they were flowers.

Taylor was all eagerness to go and see it all for himself and they left the dining-room after taking only a light pick at the main course. In the locker-room which held all the diving gear, Taylor stripped down to brief swimming trunks without a moment's hesitation. He was reaching for a wet-suit before Jillian could wrench her eyes off his magnificent body and direct her hands to her own undressing. She turned her back to Taylor as she lifted off her dress, all too conscious of what her body wanted and hoping it didn't show while she stood so terribly naked in her bikini.

She snatched up a wet-suit and dragged it on as fast as she could, feeling considerably more composed when it was zipped up. She put the necessary flippers on her feet and then Taylor was beside her, holding out the harness with the air-cylinder for her to slip her arms into. She did up the belt, still without meeting his eyes, all too aware of how the wet-suit was moulded around his muscles, making them all the more noticeable. She was glad to put on the face-mask so that her expression was less readable to him.

They each took an underwater flashlight. Jillian saw Taylor's eyes dancing at her through the clear plastic face-plate as they fitted their mouthpieces in, and then at last they lowered themselves in the water and they were in another world, one that gradually soothed Jillian's inner turbulence.

They passed shoals of tiny silver fish which turned away from them in the blink of an eyelid, the light glancing off their bodies so that they glinted iridescently for one fascinating moment and then were gone. Larger fish ignored their presence, going about their business of feeding. Their colours were not so brilliant as those seen in daytime but the endless variety of their tones was just as breathtaking.

The fabulous variety of shapes in the coral polyps

drew most of their attention ... branching antlers, plates, fans and hemispherical masses, some of them with convoluted surfaces resembling the human brain. It was a wondrous fairyland that held them captivated for the full hour that the air-tanks allowed them, and it was witn regret that they had to kick up to the surface. They took out their mouthpieces and swam slowly back to the mother-ship.

It took a tremendous effort for Jillian to haul herself up the ladder and on to the deck. She felt physically and emotionally exhausted, but, for the first time in days, her mind was at peace. The beauty she had seen overshadowed any other thought. Taylor joined her in the locker-room and they helped each other out of the diving equipment.

'That was incredible,' Taylor murmured, the wonder of their underwater experience enriching his deep voice.

Jillian slumped down on the bench seat against the wall and heaved a satisfied sigh. 'It always feels like that, every time I go down.'

And only you have moved me more, she thought in sad whimsy as she watched him drag off his flippers and strip himself of his wet-suit.

He raised an amused eyebrow at her inaction. 'Too tired to move?'

Before she could answer he was crouching at her feet, removing her flippers. The touch of his hands on her ankles and feet were electrifying enough in her weakened state of vulnerability, but when he lifted her to her feet and began unzipping her wet-suit, Jillian could hardly breathe. He slid the suit off her shoulders, pulled it down, supported her with an arm around her waist as he dragged it down her legs which he gently urged to step out of the clammy material.

There was nothing suggestive in his handling yet a sense of intimacy throbbed through her, making her tremble, and when Taylor straightened up his body was so close to hers, so close, with only a few strips of cloth separating them from total nakedness. She saw his broad chest expand as he drew in a deep breath and a few droplets of water shivered on a sprinkling of dark curls just below his throat. She could not move, could not tear her gaze away. She desperately wanted to touch him, to spread her fingers through that curly hair and feel his warm, moist skin. She wanted . . .

'Jillian . . .'

His voice sounded strange, far off, strained. She did not want to answer him, did not want to break this moment which was stretching on, becoming incredibly tense. Taylor's hands lifted. They closed over her shoulders, fingers working at her flesh as if undecided as to whether they should push her away or draw her closer. Jillian dragged her gaze up to his, wanting him to see her need and answer it, not caring about pride or humiliation or anything but her desire for him to love her in any way at all.

For only one turbulent second did she see the struggle of desire and restraint in his expression, then she was crushed against him in a fierce embrace, and his mouth was sweeping hot, feverish kisses across her temples, whispering hoarse bursts of words.

'I'll stop when you say . . . I swear I will . . . but I've got to have some of you, Jillian . . . I've got to . . . I can't stand off any longer . . .'

His hands were sweeping over her in avid possession, pressing her into the virile hardness of his body
as his kisses moved purposefully down her face,
tilting her head back.

'I've never felt such hunger for a woman,' he
breathed against her lips. 'Let me taste all of you,
Jillian. Let me . . .' An animal sound punctuated the
words as his mouth closed over hers with an urgent
sensuality which quickly changed to a wild driving
passion as she let him take whatever he wanted,
glorying in his need for her.

She felt his fingers tugging at the halter tie of her
bikini and could hardly wait for the strings to be
undone. Her breasts were tingling with anticipation,
eager for the sensation of being pressed to his bare
skin. The strings fell loose. Instinctively inviting the
brushing aside of the small triangles of cloth, Jillian
arched her back away from Taylor. His mouth left
hers, trailed down her throat. His hands ran down her
back, under her arms. She felt his body sliding down
hers and opened her eyes just as his mouth closed over
one bared breast.

He was kneeling in front of her. She clutched at his
shoulders, wildly agitated by the action, but he was
moulding her breasts with his hands, shaping them to
his mouth as he moved from one to the other, tasting
them, sucking at them, sending piercing waves of
fierce pleasure through her body. She heard strange
little cries coming from her throat and tried to steady
her breathing, but everything seemed to be out of her
control.

Then Taylor was sliding further away from her, pressing his warm lips to her stomach, licking at her navel. She grasped his head for support as her bones seemed to melt. His hands on her thighs kept her upright as he moved lower again and the moist heat of his mouth pressed through the thin nylon of her bikini briefs, his tongue probing out an intimacy that shot liquid fire into every nerve of her body.

'No . . . no . . . ' she moaned, not even knowing what she was saying as her knees buckled completely. Then somehow Taylor was on his feet, and her body was caught to his, lifted so that the sensitive place he had aroused so erotically fitted to the hard throbbing muscle of his own arousal.

'Don't say no . . . don't say no . . .' he groaned, and plundered her mouth so that she was incapable of saying anything even if she could have managed any coherent thought. She was utterly powerless against his ravaging of her senses. She was beyond any conscious decision. She was his to do with as he wished.

Then suddenly he stopped kissing her. He let her feet slide down to the floor and rested his cheek on top of her head. His breathing was fast and harsh. His arms slowly dragged out of their embrace so that only his hands grasped her hips, holding her steady.

'Forgive me,' he rasped, a shudder running through his body as he lifted his head away from hers. 'Get dressed, for God's sake!'

Jillian stared after him with glazed eyes as he lurched out to the deck and clutched the railing, his body hunched over as if fighting pain. She didn't understand. He had wanted her . . . and now he didn't want her? She shivered with a terrible sense of loss. She didn't know what to do. Taylor had ordered her to get dressed and the order kept tapping on her mind until enough strength had seeped back into her limbs to obey him. Her fingers fumbled hopelessly, but she finally managed to fasten her halter-neck bra and put her dress on.

Taylor was still leaning on the railing, his back turned to her, his head down. Her legs felt rubbery as she forced them to move but she had to go to him. She didn't understand what was happening between them and she had to know. As she stepped close to him she could see his chest heaving as he drew in deep breaths. She reached out and tentatively touched his arm.

'Taylor . . . are you all right?'

'Don't touch me!' he snapped, then seemed to recover some of his equilibrium, continuing in a more controlled but harsh voice. 'Just go, Jillian. Go back to your boat while you still have the chance.'

She felt sick from having been abandoned so abruptly at fever-pitch arousal, but his words made her feel sicker. 'Have I done something wrong?' she asked in an agonised whisper.

He gave a wild laugh that sounded as if his vocal chords were being rasped over coarse sandpaper. 'You wouldn't believe it if I told you what you've done.' His eyes flashed stormily at her. 'I'll give you three seconds to get on your way, Jillian. If you stay here any longer I'm going to take you down to my cabin and do what I'm trying to restrain myself from doing.'

He did still want her, Jillian thought exultantly.

Taylor's eyes glinted with dangerous fire. His teeth gritted. 'One . . .'

Jillian stared at him, mesmerised by the naked desire that looked back at her. Desire, not love, her mind appraised slowly. Not once had Taylor spoken of love. He wanted her badly but . . .

'Two . . .'

Did it matter? her heart whispered yearningly. If she gave him all of herself . . . and finished up with emotional emptiness . . .

'Three!'

She turned and fled, running for the safety and security of *Dreamcatcher*, her body protesting at every step but her mind dictating them, relentlessly telling her that there had to be more from Taylor than the passing pleasure that his body could give her.

But escape brought her no consolation. In the loneliness of the night, the sense of being bereft that burrowed into Jillian's heart declared her mind a traitor to the love she bore for Taylor Marshall. It was not as if Taylor felt nothing but desire for her. Hadn't he been showing her for days that her company meant more to him than the physical satisfaction of having sex with her?

Even tonight, when she couldn't have refused him, he had backed off, freeing her of pressure so that she could make her own decision. It had hurt him but he had still done it, for her sake. He had cared about what she thought and felt, more than following through on what he had wanted from her. And she had run away again!

Jillian writhed over the missed opportunity of showing Taylor that she loved him. So he had not spoken of love to her! She had not spoken of love to him, either. And what was he thinking of her now, leaving him like that when she had virtually invited his lovemaking? Why did she always have to go and mess everything up with him?

The answer was all too obvious. It was because everything mattered so much and she had no control over it. She was frightened of the power that Taylor had over her life. She knew that he could either give her the greatest happiness or the most terrible despair. And there was so little time left to resolve that question. Tomorrow was the second last day.

CHAPTER SEVEN

IT was a perfect day. The sun climbed into a cloudless sky and beat down upon the water so that it looked more opalescent than turquoise around the coral cay. The sea was completely calm. Even the ocean swell which had travelled halfway around the world from the South American coast seemed diminished. Frigate birds and terns wheeled and glided effortlessly through the air in search of their breakfast.

Jillian looked at them with a jaundiced eye. They appeared free and happy, supremely content with their lot in life. She was not, and probably never would feel that way again. Just two more days and Taylor Marshall would be gone and her life would seem utterly meaningless because the most important part of it would have been lost.

A shout caught their attention. Taylor was hailing them from the mother-ship to come over and collect him. It was much earlier than he usually came aboard, and Jillian's heart jiggled between pleasure and uncertainty. Did he want to be with her? Every minute with him was so precious now, yet she was apprehensive about his reaction to her after last night. Would he count it as another rejection and stay with the men today?

Just the sight of him emphasised the hopelessness of her own cause. He was so handsome, so virile and

124

charming that every woman he met probably wanted to go to bed with him. And Jillian knew she was no one special. His interest in her undoubtedly sprang from the fact that she was here, on hand, and reasonably attractive.

She would be forgotten once he was back in America where there had to be thousands of pretty, talented women who would suit him much better than her; women of similar background to himself, women who knew and understood his kind of life, women who could easily cope with whatever he wanted. Yet when he climbed on board *Dreamcatcher* he gave Jillian a smile that wiped every dubious thought from her mind and filled her with happiness.

'Morning, Jillian,' he said in a voice that harboured no recriminations.

Her smile beamed joyful relief at him. 'Good morning, Taylor.'

'Glad to see you up and about, me lad,' old George put in. 'Are your offsiders ready? We need to be on our way.'

Taylor grinned at him. 'A touch of arthritis got you on the move early today, George?'

'An itch between me shoulder-blades,' old George said succinctly and stared dreamily out to sea. 'Always happens when there's big marlin around. Really big.'

Taylor nodded to Bob. 'Better go and collect the others then, Bob. And tell Jerry to bring plenty of film. George says so,' he added with a laughing look at Jillian which shared her confidence in the old skipper's predictions.

'Where are we going to, George?' she asked happily.

He was a long time answering, his gaze sweeping the sea and following the flight of the birds. 'Reckon we might try Escape or Agincourt,' he said musingly.

'I've never known big fish off there,' Jillian commented questioningly.

He kept watching the birds then nodded a few times. 'That's where we'll try. Go get the engines warmed up, Jilly.'

She raised her eyebrows at Taylor who spread his hands in a carefree gesture, then waved her up the ladder. He followed on her heels, and his closeness sent her pulse-rate sky-rocketing again. He still wanted to be with her. He had even come over early to be with her. And he held no grudge about last night. Her heart was singing as she started up the engines.

Taylor did not sit down. He stood beside her and, when she glanced up at him, the expression in his eyes was warm enough to send melting tremors through her body. 'I didn't mean to upset you last night, Jillian,' he said with soft sincerity.

'You didn't,' she said quickly, every instinct clamouring to prevent Taylor from retreating into the role of friend again. She didn't want him as a friend. She wanted him as a lover for the rest of her life.

He sighed and a funny little self-mocking smile curled his mouth. 'I was trying to win your trust and ended up forcing you to run away from me again. I didn't want that, Jillian. I hope . . .'

'It's all right, Taylor,' she rushed in recklessly,

then blushed at her forwardness. 'I ... I wanted you to kiss me.' She dropped her gaze, knowing that she wanted so much more from him than a kiss and still afraid of what such a total surrender might mean.

'But not like that,' Taylor murmured and gently lifted her chin. 'Like this ...'

His mouth on hers was soft, caring, and Jillian instinctively turned to him, welcoming his kiss and responding to it with tumultuous joy. Yet Taylor did not take advantage of her eager pliancy. His arms wrapped her in a slow, tender embrace, as if she was fragile and precious. His lips moved over hers with a slow, searching carefulness that wanted to give reassurance rather than arouse excitement but Jillian was giddy with the emotions he stirred by the time he drew back.

'Better?' he asked, and there was a strained note in his voice which suggested he was exerting the utmost control.

'Yes,' she whispered huskily, denying her own urge to throw herself at him.

The putter of the outboard motor on the dinghy intruded on the moment, drawing Taylor's attention away from her. He threw a glance towards the mother-ship then smiled down at her. 'Then I won't press my luck. I want you to be happy with me today.'

She was almost bursting with happiness. Taylor took his usual seat beside her and stayed with her all the way to Escape Reef. He didn't even bother to go down to the cockpit when they started trolling. She didn't care if they never caught a fish. Their phenomenal success throughout the charter had ensured that *Dreamcatcher* would be lead boat for some time and she didn't want Taylor to leave her side today. Jillian hoped that he felt the same way, that there was so little time left to them that every possible moment had to be shared.

They talked of silly little happy things. Taylor commented on the trolling patterns and used the boat to demonstrate football plays on the water. No one sighted a fish, and Jillian wondered if old George had deliberately brought them to barren fishing grounds so that she and Taylor could have the time together. It didn't matter. She didn't care what anyone thought. She only cared about Taylor staying with her.

Lunchtime came. Old George suggested she move on to Agincourt. It was only a small trip and Jillian soon had the boat in its trolling pattern again. However, when Taylor would have rejoined her on the fly-bridge after lunch, Earl Schultz chided him over the time he had spent aloft with Jillian.

'If George reckons there's big marlin around here, today might be the day when you can catch a world record, and how are you going to do that from up there? At least give yourself a chance, Taylor.'

Taylor glanced up at Jillian, made a resigned grimace, then dropped down into the cockpit again. 'OK, I'll give it a chance for an hour or two,' he acceded good-naturedly.

Disappointment clouded Jillian's spirits. It seemed a waste of time trolling these waters if Taylor wasn't going to sit with her. They might as well go where the fish were really running. She was almost sure that old George had deliberately given them a bum steer. The exultant call from him snapped her out of her brooding reverie.

'Fish up!'

She jerked her head around, knowing instantly she had made a bad mistake. From her position she should have seen the fish first not old George. She caught a glimpse of a huge mass charging through the water and that was all before the line was screaming from the reel. Taylor leapt for the chair. He seized the rod and was heaving back with all his might as Bob was still trying to fasten the seat-harness on him. 'Go!' he yelled, and Jillian gunned the motors to effect the hook-up.

The fish did not come out of the water. It headed for the horizon at a speed which almost outran the boat, taking most of the line with it. The difficulty for Jillian lay in judging the tension on the line. If she went too slowly the line might run out before Taylor achieved some mastery over the fish's direction, but too fast and the margin for error in the slack became unacceptable. She concentrated fiercely, determined to give Taylor every possible chance. Even over the sound of the engines she could hear him grunting with the effort of putting pressure on the fish.

It took the best part of an hour and a half to recover half of the line. In the hot afternoon sunshine Taylor's body was lathered with sweat. Every time they gained substantially on the fish it took off on another murderous run. Taylor was working harder than Jillian had ever seen an angler work. The tension around the boat was palpable. Whatever this fish was, marlin or shark, it was huge and powerful. Old

George was throwing buckets of water over the reel to counteract the heat generated from the long runs of Dacron line.

It was into the third hour before they saw it. It broke water in an earthshaking rush. It was the biggest marlin Jillian had ever seen, so awesome in its size that it seemed as big as the boat. Jerry Somers worked overtime on his camera as the mighty fish tail-walked along the water, twisting, turning, gyrating in its drive to break free of the hook. Twenty yards it went ... fifty ... a hundred ... a hundred and fifty ... further than any fish in Jillian's memory ... defying gravity in its fearsome acrobatics.

'There's your record if you're good enough to catch it, lad,' old George threw at Taylor. 'A few hundred pounds over anything that's been caught, if I'm any judge.'

Taylor's only answer was another grunt. The others were too stunned to comment. And suddenly the fish turned and made straight for them. Jillian hit the throttles again. Taylor reeled in like a madman. The marlin was within a hundred yards of them, the tension still being sustained on the line, and the fish was slowing down.

'You've got it! You've got it!' Earl shouted in gleeful encouragement.

But as if the fish sensed the imminent danger, it made another bid for freedom. It turned and went deep, plunging to the floor of the ocean. Jillian drove the boat in circling patterns while Taylor fought for inches of line. Every muscle of his body was strained to the limit, and, with a pang of disappointment for him, Jillian realised that the fight was going on too long. He would weaken first, not that giant of a fish.

The marlin lay at least a hundred feet under the water surface. Taylor's fingers were gripped white on rod and reel and she could hear his groans of effort as he tried to raise the enormous fish. An inch or two of progress was made, and then nothing. Jillian imagined the great pectoral fins of the marlin spread out on the ocean floor, acting like a brake to any pressure applied. The only way that great fish was going to be raised was with a crane. It was beyond any single human being's capacity.

The fight had been going on for over four hours. Jillian's heart ached with sympathy for Taylor. He had tried so hard. She knew how much he would want to succeed, how much any angler would, but he was strained to the limit and it could not go on like this. The unequal contest had to be ended one way or another and the only way Jillian could see was to take the responsibility herself.

'Hold it there, Taylor,' she called out. 'I've got a plan.'

A sense of detachment came over her as the other men in the cockpit lifted curious faces.

'There's no way you're going to lift that fish and I'm not going to have it die down there. So . . .' She took a deep breath, knowing the plan was completely unorthodox. 'I'm going to back off to about three-quarters of your line, then swing the boat so that it puts a belly in the line between you and fish. That will change the angle you're trying to take the fish on and maybe it'll make the marlin change its position, draw it up to us.'

'You can't do it, Jilly,' George rumbled at her. 'No one can put a belly in a line and get away with it. You'll lose the fish.'

'Has it been tried before?' Jillian asked.

'No, because everyone knows that's the surest way of losing a fish,' old George shot back at her.

'Taylor can't draw it up and it'll die down there, George. We'll lose it anyway,' she argued.

'Jilly, it's a world record for sure!'

'Only if you catch it,' she retorted.

'No! Give him a chance.'

It was easy for onlookers to say that, Jillian thought fiercely as she once more observed the physical exhaustion that was written all over the man in the fighting-chair. 'I'm the skipper, George,' she said stubbornly. 'Are you ready, Taylor?'

There were cries of protest from the others but Jillian only looked at Taylor and he slowly nodded assent. She drove the boat away from the marlin, checking that the line was steady. She knew that she was giving up all the line that Taylor had struggled so valiantly for hours to recover, and if her scheme didn't work, she would have to shoulder all the blame for the loss of the fish, but she was convinced that any other course would have resulted in failure anyway.

The moment of decision came and, with her nerves tingling with apprehension, Jillian slowly turned the boat. Taylor held the rod steady. He did not reel in as the line gradually formed an arc. He was trusting her judgment and Jillian hoped with all her heart that the

plan would work for him. For the first time in too
many hours, the line was no longer taut. She felt the
disbelief on the other men's faces, felt the waves of
scepticism and disappointment, but she did not look
at them. She was watching the line.

Nothing happened. With mounting dismay she
wished the fish would cut the line and go free and this
whole terrible business would be over. Suddenly the
arc of the line dropped lower. The fish had stirred. It
was on the move, following the line. Bob and old
George were screaming at Taylor to reel in. He
reeled, not even bothering to pump the rod. Jillian
manoeuvred the boat, increasing the angle of the arc a
fraction more.

The fish broke the water again in a cataclysm of
spray, a spectacle of primitive grandeur as its huge
bulk shook itself against the sky, its mighty bill
spearing the air in wild defiance.

'That's two thousand pounds if I'm a day,' old
George crowed in excitement.

Taylor had reeled in the slack and they were
gaining rapidly on the marlin now. It was tired, not so
full of fight any more.

'Outers, Bob!' Jillian yelled. 'Don't forget your
outers!'

He waved up at her, showing he had already put the
cotton gloves on. But his face wasn't smiling any
more. It was tense. The giant marlin was close and it
was big and dangerous, liable to fight capture all the
way. The wire leader came out of the water. If the fish
rushed them from here, its bill could go through the
boat as if it was matchwork. It could stab Taylor to

death. It had been done before. Jillian knew she held all their lives in their hands. Everything depended on a split-second reaction with the controls if the marlin charged. Her hands were trembling. A lump of fear caught the breath in her throat.

Bob grabbed the wire. He began hauling it in, wrapping it around the outer gloves which could be so quickly discarded if necessary. She could see the springy tension in his body. He was ready for any move.

'Tag it.'

The words were slurred and barely comprehensible, shaped from the parched lips of Taylor Marshall. Jillian couldn't believe her ears. No one tagged a world record fish!

There were startled reactions from everyone.

'Don't be a fool!' Earl Schultz cried.

'Taylor, you can't claim a record unless it's weighed under IGFA rules,' old George expostulated.

'She's coming in!' Bob urged him on anxiously.

'No one'll believe us, honour sport or not!' Earl pleaded.

'I've got it all on film,' Jerry Somers put in, eyeing the marlin uneasily.

The fish was coming in. There seemed no fight left in it but its sheer size was ominously dangerous. Bob kept on wrapping the wire around his hand. Foot by foot the massive marlin was drawn inexorably closer. There was an electric silence, eyes shifting imploringly from the fish to Taylor and back again. The man in the fighting-chair looked completely spent, too weary to make a decision. But he made it.

'I said . . . tag it.' The words were choked, ragged.

George looked at Taylor as if he was mad.

Taylor's head came up and he stared George down. 'It's the angler's decision. Tag it!' he ordered with the explosiveness of a tortured breath.

'Holy mother of God!' George muttered as he reached back for the tagging pole. 'A man waits a lifetime . . .'

But Jillian felt no regret. An intense jubilation burst into her heart as old George drove the tag into the side of the fish, a mere pin-prick in its mighty body. His hands were shaking as he withdrew the pole. Bob cut the wire with his pliers. For one moment the fish lay passively, its brain not immediately registering that it had been released. Then with a great swish of its tale the giant marlin took a leap for freedom, the red colour of anger already fading from its body as it tore through the water, merging with the iridescent blue of its natural habitat. It was gone so fast that the whole experience seemed like a dream. The scene on the boat was a frozen tableau of people, staring out at nothing but the sea.

Jillian recovered first. She slammed the controls into neutral and rushed down the ladder, throwing all restraint to the winds. She shoved past old George who was still in a daze, rubbing his fingers through the few strands of hair on his head and muttering to everyone and no one, 'I'll be damned.' Taylor was slumped in the fighting-chair, too prostrate to respond to anything, but she kissed him over and over, telling him he was marvellous and all sorts of incoherent things.

He gave her a travesty of a smile. 'I'm done in, honey,' he croaked.

He winced as she took the rod out of his hands and replaced it in its slot. There were blisters on his palms. She slid her arms around his back as he leaned forward and did her best to support him as he heaved himself out of the chair. For a few rocky moments they both staggered until Earl Schultz lent a steadying hand.

'You all right, Taylor?' he asked belatedly.

'I'm taking him into my cabin,' Jillian stated in her best authoritative tone. 'He needs medication on those hands and a thorough rub-down.'

'I'm not that bad,' Taylor muttered.

'Shut up and lean on me,' Jillian ordered.

'I'll be double-damned!' old George murmured and clapped a hand on Bob's shoulder. 'Well, somebody had better drive the boat. Up you go, Bob. Steer about a hundred and fifty-five degrees.' He shook his head again. 'I still can't believe it.'

'I've got it on film, George,' Jerry Somers reminded him. 'We can show it to the other guys on the mother-ship tonight. I bet it'll blow their minds.'

'Mine's already blown,' Earl Schultz remarked mournfully. 'I can't believe he let it go. He had it. He had it right there. Didn't he?'

Jillian manoeuvred Taylor into her cabin and shut the door on the stunned voices. She swept the blanket off her bunk so that he could lie down on the cool sheet and helped him off with his T-shirt. She left him for a minute or two while she mixed him a long cold drink of mineral water and Staminade, and grabbed some ointment and deep-heat liniment from the medicine box. Taylor drank with the thirst of a man brought in from the desert.

'Want some more?' she asked anxiously.

He collapsed back on to the pillow and moved his head in a negative fashion. She spread ointment over the blisters and as she finished one hand and started on the other, he trailed his fingers lightly down her arm. 'You wanted me to let it go, didn't you?'

She met his tired gaze with eyes that were luminous with a great welling of love. He had done it for her. He had given up his world record for her. 'Oh, Taylor!' she breathed ecstatically. 'I just wanted whatever you wanted.' And she kissed him with a poignant tenderness that came straight from her soul.

His arms came around her in a rough embrace. 'Lie with me, Jillian,' he murmured huskily.

She kissed him again, softly, lingeringly. 'Not yet, Taylor. I want you to turn over so I can give you a rub-down. You'll be so stiff and sore if I don't.'

He gave her a rueful smile. 'I guess you're right. Just don't leave me, mmh?'

'No chance,' she promised fervently. She squeezed the liniment out on his shoulders and, after a moment's hesitation, climbed up on the bunk and knelt astride him as she worked on his muscles, rubbing and kneading. She found the action uncomfortably erotic at first, but she quickly dismissed her inhibitions and let herself enjoy the pleasure of feeling his firm body beneath hers.

She lost all sense of time as she worked on him, revelling in the ripple of his muscles under her hands. She had to force herself to turn around and begin on his thighs but that was just as exciting, nerve-shatteringly so when he moved them apart for easier massage.

'Do you know what you're doing to me?' he groaned into the pillow.

A surge of heat tingled through Jillian's body. 'Relax,' she admonished him breathlessly.

'I can smell the scent of your hair on this pillow. I want . . .' He gave a shuddering sigh as Jillian stroked down his inner thighs. 'God almighty! I can't take much more.'

'I only have to do the calf-muscles now,' Jillian said just as raggedly. Her own thoughts were running rampant with images of their bodies moving together.

Neither of them noticed the engines die, nor were they aware that the boat was becalmed. The knock on the cabin door came as a rude shock. 'Taylor, we're back at the mother-ship,' Earl Schultz called out.

'Tell him to go to hell,' Taylor growled into the pillow, but Jillian had already hopped off the bunk in a guilty rush.

'You can't. They'll want you with them to talk about the fish,' she gabbled.

Taylor grabbed her arm as she would have reached for the door. His eyes were ablaze with the need which was shivering through her own body. His fingers closed tightly around her wrist, regardless of his blisters, and for a moment it seemed he would not be denied. Then the fire softened as he took in the self-conscious alarm in her eyes and he sighed. 'You'll come over to the mother-ship tonight? I want you to be with me, Jillian.'

She nodded.

'Be out in a minute, Earl,' he barked and reluctantly heaved himself off the bunk. He kissed her, long and deeply, pressing the whole length of her body to his in yearning urgency. 'Don't keep me waiting too long, honey-girl,' he whispered, then pulled back and shone a wide grin at her. 'I might last out an hour while you let out your hair from that plait and put on your sexy blue dress.'

'It's not sexy,' she denied shakily.

His grin grew wider. 'Honey, there's not a damned thing you don't look sexy in to me. One hour. No more,' he warned, and left her to join Earl and Jerry for the trip over to the mother-ship.

CHAPTER EIGHT

EVERYONE gathered into the saloon to watch the video again. It had been played before dinner and had been the subject of all conversation over dinner, and there was not a soul on board the mother-ship that was not alight with eagerness to see that mighty marlin again. The news of a world record catch had quickly spread to all the fleet and boats had come streaming in, their crews and charters swelling the numbers so that the spacious saloon was crammed with people.

There were gasps of awe and disbelief as the fish seemed to burst out of the screen on its long tail-walk across the water, but the most telling film sequence was that of the marlin being hauled in by Bob. Its size in comparison to the boat drew amazed comments and a concert of declarations that old George had certainly been right in his estimate . . . a world record for sure.

'And who'd be doubting me word?' old George rolled out at them over his umpteenth glass of whisky.

Over the rollicking laughter which ensued, one incredulous voice asked the question, 'Why on earth did you tag it?'

Eyes turned to Taylor Marshall and he gave a dry, whimsical smile. 'So that it would still be out there waiting for one of you guys to catch it, and give you the pleasure and excitement it gave me,' he answered

140

simply, but his eyes twinkled at Jillian, giving her a more intimate answer.

For a moment there was dead silence around the room then someone proposed three cheers for Taylor Marshall and the saloon rang with hearty jubilation. Bottles of champagne were opened at an astonishing rate and glass after glass was pressed on to Taylor and Jillian, everyone wanting to congratulate the angler who had displayed such skill and stamina as to stay with such a fish and reel it in, and the skipper who had dared unconventional means to raise the fish for its eventual capture.

Jillian found the congratulations heady stuff, and the champagne even headier, but neither was as exhilarating as being at Taylor Marshall's side, sharing his moment of glory and knowing he wanted her with him. He didn't even seem interested in the glory. His hand moved restlessly on hers, gripping, stroking, caressing. Every time she met his gaze his eyes held hers, softly probing, asking, wanting.

The celebration was just getting into full swing when Taylor steered her out of the saloon. The party had spilled on to the decks of the mother-ship and it was clear that any privacy was out of the question. 'Come down to my cabin,' Taylor whispered to her. 'It's the only place on the boat that we can be alone and I want to spend what little time we have left with you.'

'Yes. Please,' she rushed out ingenuously, way beyond hiding her desire to be alone with him, too.

They stole away from the crowd and Taylor closed his cabin door behind them with a sigh of relief. The room was small but compared to Jillian's tiny cabin on *Dreamcatcher* it was positively luxurious. Discreet light fittings cast a rich glow on the polished timber walls and the gold and orange bedspread, which was all Jillian saw before Taylor was turning her, his hands slipping around her waist.

'I'm dead-beat, honey,' he murmured, gently kissing her forehead. 'Come and lie down with me?'

'Would you rather I go and let you sleep?' she asked anxiously.

'Hell, no,' he said emphatically, drawing her with him as he flopped on to the bed.

Jillian was sprawled half across him as they landed and Taylor grinned at her, his eyes sparkling teasingly through lazily lowered lids. 'I'm at your mercy. Want to have your way with me?'

She laughed, more from a nervous thrill of excitement than amusement. She quite desperately wanted to have her way with him but wasn't at all sure how to go about it. Her love for him needed physical expression and the memory of this afternoon's massage burned through her mind. Taylor had been excited by her touch. For days she had ached to touch him and now he was giving her the opportunity, maybe the last opportunity she would have, if she had the courage to take it.

She pulled herself up to kneel at his side. He looked at her with happy, tired eyes and she loved him, loved him beyond every inhibition that had kept her own desires suppressed. She leaned forward and gently brushed the hair from his forehead. Her fingers slowly traced all the contours of his handsome face, across his broad forehead, along his hairline, around his eyes, the high cheekbones and the hard plane of his jawline, to the soft sensuality of his mouth.

Taylor had closed his eyes at her first touch but she was aware of his utter stillness, the tension of his held breath. Her fingers slid back up to his temples as she pressed her mouth to his and she felt the leap of his pulse as she licked her tongue between his lips. He opened them with a choked gasp and she sensed the enormous control he was exerting to remain passive as she kissed him slowly, experimentally, savouring the incredible eroticism of doing whatever she wished while sensing his barely leashed excitement.

His arms encircled her, inexorably drawing her body down to meet his. A hand slid around to cup the fullness of her breast and the soft, tingling pressure made her unfold her legs to seek a more intimate contact with him. His hands stroked down her spine, grasped her hips and pulled her lower body over his own, her legs falling to either side of his. The hard, urgent pressure that met her softness touched off alarms in her head. She should stop now. But she didn't want to leave him and her heart over-ruled her head. She would give Taylor whatever he wanted of her, and give herself the full wonder of knowing all of him.

She slid her hand down the firm column of his throat which felt as tense now as the hard, muscular body under her. She flicked open his shirt buttons and spread her fingers through the springy curls of hair she had wanted to touch last night. She could do it now. She could do anything now. The warmth of his skin, the different male texture of it, sent shivers of pleasure through her fingertips. She explored further.

Suddenly Taylor tore her hands away from him. His chest heaved under her and he rolled, pinning her beneath him, his thighs between hers, her arms slammed up above her head so that her breasts were stretched tautly against his chest while he kissed her with violent passion, again and again, ravaging her mouth in a fierce need to possess. Her lips were bruised and throbbing and her breath coming in tortured gasps when he finally lifted his head away.

'Don't tease me, Jillian,' he rasped, his breath as tortured as her own.

Then he released her hands. His body left hers. She opened dazed eyes to find him kneeling back on his haunches, his face contorted with restrained passion, his eyes dark pools of need as they roved over her thighs still spread in abandonment to him. Her heart melted with love for him. He was letting her go, giving her the chance to go, even now when she had no defences left.

'I'm not teasing.' Her voice was rough with her own need. 'I want you to touch me, Taylor. I want to touch you.'

He stared down at her, eyes glittering feverishly. 'You really want me, Jillian? Are you sure?' The words were deeply guttural, torn from a throat that was choked with desire.

'Yes,' she whispered. More than anything else in the world, I want you, Taylor Marshall, her heart added with silent yearning.

He reached out, fingertips brushing tentatively

along her thigh. She quivered under his touch and he withdrew it, lifting a trembling hand to rake through his hair. He sucked in a sharp breath and dragged his gaze back to hers. 'No more running away?'

She shook her head but still he didn't come to her. He tore his shirt off, and sat there, his hands on his own powerful thighs as he drew in several deep breaths. 'I want to take you now, but it wouldn't be enough,' he muttered hoarsely. 'I need to have all of you, Jillian. Every last inch of you as mine. Does that frighten you?'

A wild, primitive tremor of exultation ran through her at the raw declaration of his need. She saw a fine sheen of sweat break out on the well-developed muscles of his shoulders and chest and she wanted to reach up and run her hands over them but she sensed that any movement on her part might trigger the explosive power that Taylor was so obviously struggling to hold in.

'I want all of you, too,' she confessed huskily.

A triumphant fire flashed from his eyes, igniting a tremulous heat inside her as he leaned forward and pulled the bow at her waist undone. His hands shook a little as he caressed the bodice of her dress from her shoulders and gathered her up to him so that he could unfasten her bra. He kissed her with long, drugging kisses, then gently but firmly untwined her arms from his neck and lay her down, sliding both dress and bra from her arms.

His gaze travelled slowly over her naked torso, drinking in her soft femininity with an avidity that was as exciting as his kisses. Jillian's nipples tingled into prominence and he bent over and ran his tongue around each areola. She grasped his shoulders and arched towards him, shivering with the pleasure he was giving her and aching to give him everything.

But again he pulled away from her and his eyes held an exultant glitter as they swept over her throbbing breasts. In one fluid movement he was off the bed and stripping her of dress and panties. He pushed his trousers down over taut, lean hips, and when he straightened naked before her, Jillian's eyes fixed in mesmerised wonder on the sheer power emanating from his manhood. He was beautiful. A man amongst men. And he was hers. She reached out and touched him and his whole body jerked cataleptically, throwing into sharp relief every finely honed muscle.

A guttural cry tore from his throat and he convulsively gripped her hand there as he knelt over her.

He looked magnificent and Jillian was so intoxicated with her love for him she uninhibitedly showed him so, revelling in being able to excite him into groans of pleasure, doing whatever he asked, elated with her power to excite him, wanting to possess him more intimately than any woman before her so that he would forget them all and only want her.

As if driven by the same desire, Taylor stamped his own possession on her body in a frenzy of passion, kissing her breasts to such swollen sensitivity that Jillian moaned from the exquisite pleasure of it. His mouth grazed across her stomach and the melting ache inside her became a tension which demanded some release. He caressed her thighs into quivering expectancy then moved his head lower, probing the most incredible intimacy with his tongue.

Jillian cried out from the sheer shock of the excitement that shot along her nerves, racking her body in an exquisite torture that demanded release. Her hands scrabbled over his shoulders in protest, tore through his hair, completely beyond control as her body undulated in an agony of wanting. Words spilled out, begging, pleading incoherencies that Taylor ignored until her whole body was suffused with a molten heat.

Only then did he raise himself up and she grasped for him. A cry of urgency broke from his lips and he descended on her with a fierceness that could know no denial. The tearing pain only lasted a fraction of a second. Taylor gasped harshly, seemed to hesitate, but even as her fingers dug into the small of his back to press him further into her, he was doing so. She arched her back in total abandonment to him, wanting, needing the pressure of his chest against her breasts. Her head was tossing from side to side in mindless conjunction with the instinctive movement of her hips.

He stilled her head with his hands and kissed her, a soft, breathless kiss which was oddly tender at such a moment. His lips parted from hers with a soft moan of need and his arms slid around her, hugging her to him in fierce possession. He began to move inside her, a careful, strangely voluptuous kind of rotation that banished any trace of discomfort, replacing it with warm gushes of unbelievable excitement.

As the rhythmic strokes became more urgent, a

wild, primitive exhilaration drove her body to welcome each powerful thrust of her man with a passionate joy. The throes of ecstasy drenched her body. She kissed him with uninhibited fervour, stroked him with recklessly urging hands, and felt a wanton triumph when he went completely out of control, his breath rasping in short gasps, every muscle strained to bursting point until at last he found release in her, shuddering in violent spasms and crying out his own ultimate surrender of self.

Jillian felt complete in a way she had never before imagined possible, utterly sated with a sense of wondrous fulfilment. Taylor collapsed on her and in the same movement rolled her with him on to their sides so that his weight would not be oppressive. He cradled her so closely that there was no separation and they clung together in a long, languorous silence that was more eloquent of their need for each other than any speech.

Everything felt so right. Jillian knew that no other man could ever give her so much joy and pleasure. Her eyes roved dreamily over his face, completely relaxed now, a soft curve of contentment on his lips, and she loved him so fiercely, so totally, so possessively, that she felt certain now that he loved her just as deeply. It had to be so.

Eventually Taylor's breathing became slow and heavy and Jillian reluctantly wriggled her leg out from under him so that they might settle more comfortably. His eyes opened slowly, filled with drowsy contentment. Jillian smiled her pleasure at him. He was so handsome, so devastatingly handsome. He had surely made love to many, many girls in all his years as a top professional football player, but that didn't matter one bit so long as he loved her.

'Happy now?' he drawled softly.

'Mmm . . .' She snuggled closer to him, blissfully happy. Life couldn't be more perfect.

He rolled on to his back, flinging an arm over the other side of the bed. He lay staring up at the ceiling, his body stretched out in complete relaxation. Jillian wished he hadn't moved away from her but she realised that their lovemaking must have left him completely drained, coming on top of such an exhausting day. And he had loved her. He surely did love her. That was the only important thing.

'What are you thinking?' she asked, fairly certain of the reply she wanted to hear.

He rolled towards her and propped himself up on one elbow. He lifted his other hand and his fingers gently traced the outline of her lips. 'Touchdown,' he murmured with a smile that held a wealth of satisfaction.

A ripple of shock blanked out her mind. 'W . . . w . . . what?' she stammered.

His lids were half-closed, the narrowed eyes dark with weariness, but the smile on his face broadened to a chuckle of contentment. 'Don't look so stunned, honey-girl. Every man has his pride. You've been running from me since the first day I met you, and nothing meant more to me than catching you. To have this with you, it was even worth while giving up a world record.'

He slid an arm under her shoulders and dropped

back on to the pillow, pulling her across his chest so that her head rested over his heart. Jillian didn't resist. It was pointless now, but all the magic had gone out of their togetherness. She felt numb all over. His fingers entwined in her long hair. He drew in a deep breath and spoke in slurring weariness. 'You really weren't very experienced with men.'

'No.'

If he felt or heard the ice in her voice he gave no indication of it. His chest heaved a contented sigh. 'That's a gift I'll treasure in my memory, all my life.'

Oh yes! A 'touchdown' in virgin territory was undoubtedly a scalp on his belt he might like to remember, particularly when it had required so much devious skill to achieve. A swell of bitterness choked any reply to him and while Jillian's mind whirled in a fearful treadmill of agonising thoughts, the slow, rhythmic rise and fall of Taylor's chest told her he had drifted into a deep sleep.

A terrible chill seeped through her body, dispelling every last vestige of the heat of love. She had given herself to Taylor Marshall in love, but he had taken her out of pride. Pride! He had told her she would succumb to him before the end of the charter, and she had. He had taken up the challenge she had thrown at him so unwittingly . . . the one that got away . . . and he had seen it through to this end. He had got her. He had her still.

She shivered and eased away from him, curling herself into a tight, lonely ball on the edge of the bed. She remembered his terrible anger on those first two dinner dates, the murderous rage of his wounded

male ego. She should have known he would not forget
nor forgive so quickly. She had been a fool and he had
played her for a fool. Not only that, he had played her
like a fish, using exactly the same ploys as he had used
today with the giant marlin.

Her response to him those first couple of nights had
told him all too plainly that he had struck deep. She
had run, but he could have had no doubts that the
hook of his attraction had remained firm when he
made his offer of friendship and it was accepted so
promptly. The long days and nights of being the
perfect gentleman had been just like putting a belly in
the line, lulling her into moving towards him. He had
almost reeled her in last night, then deliberately let
her run again because seduction was not the triumph
he wanted. Oh no! His pride would only be satisfied
with whole-hearted surrender. The release of the
world record marlin had been for her all right . . . a
master-stroke of brilliant implications . . . and she had
fallen for it, hook, line and sinker.

With growing nausea she recalled his hesitations
over her willingness to stay with him tonight, the
careful questions that she had seen as loving care for
her but that were, in reality, a calculated means to
evoke an unequivocal surrender from her. He had
cleverly dispensed with every possible reservation and
then taken all she had to give him. He had stripped
her naked, body and soul, completely ravaged every
intimacy from her so that nothing had escaped him.
And his pride . . . his pride had been avenged!

And she was left with nothing. A grey, frozen
emptiness stretched through her soul. She wanted to

die, to be as dead as the love which had shrivelled into bleak nothingness, but her heart kept beating its mournful toll of life. And little by little a sliver of bitter light crept into her dark despair. She did have something left. She had her pride! If it was the last thing she ever did she would slap Taylor Marshall's victory back in his face.

She straightened her cold limbs and forced herself off his bed. She dressed herself with grim care and let herself quietly out of the cabin. The sounds of revelry above sounded tinnily in her ears. With bitter irony she realised the celebration party was still going on. Three cheers for Taylor Marshall, she thought savagely, the best angler in all waters, especially skilled in mastering female fishes!

She found old George slumped in an armchair, an empty bottle of whisky in his hand. He was clearly beyond operating his feet by himself. She found Bob in the middle of a boisterous group on the aft-deck, and together they managed to get the old skipper into the dinghy. Bob steered them across to *Dreamcatcher*, helped Jillian to get old George on to his bunk, then departed to rejoin the party.

Jillian wandered back out to the cockpit and sat in the fighting-chair. She thought about Taylor for a long, long time, and eventually she formed a plan which satisfied her, satisfied every festering wound he had scored on her pride. Then she went to bed, knowing precisely how she would deal with tomorrow. Tomorrow and Taylor Marshall.

CHAPTER NINE

IT was another perfect day, but Jillian was in no mood to appreciate it. She was too miserable to appreciate anything, but her mind burnt with one fierce resolution . . . that Taylor Marshall was not going to enjoy his triumph over her. The man had to be an egomaniac, and she castigated herself over and over again for having misjudged him so badly. A new-born cynicism made her wonder if all famous people were like that, but her contact with the celebrities who came to Cairns had been too slight for her to make a general judgment.

Thankfully she didn't have to make small talk with Bob and old George; both were suffering from monumental hangovers. Bob had spread himself out in the sun on the fore-deck, trying to sweat out the lingering effects of alcohol; old George was nursing his head over yet another mug of black coffee. He groaned and snuffled into his beard. Jillian eyed him unsympathetically. She wasn't feeling sympathetic to any male this morning.

'You brought it all on yourself, George,' she snapped at him uncharacteristically.

'Now, don't be taking that tone with me, lass,' he moaned, and looked up at her balefully. 'I had to do it.'

'Rubbish!' she bit out, then tried to take a hold on

herself. Her world might be falling about but she shouldn't be taking out her hurt on others, particularly old George who had never done her any harm.

'God's truth!' he slurred insistently. 'I swore my oath on two bottles of whisky and last night I had to unswear it.' He shook his head dolefully. 'When a slip of a girl like you, and an amateur like Taylor Marshall, can show me something about fishing, it's about time I made a comeback. Show every young smart-aleck what I can do. I'm going to be skipper for the rest of the season, lass. You can go back to your dress shop.'

Jillian sagged with relief, then rushed over to give the old skipper an affectionate hug. 'You don't know how much that means to me. Thank you, George,' she breathed gratefully. She kissed his stragglyhaired head again and again in an excess of gratitude.

'Now, now, Jilly,' he reproved her gently. 'You can be saving that for the man himself.'

She drew away as bitterness squeezed her heart. 'If you mean Taylor Marshall,' she said coldly, 'he won't be getting any more from me.'

Old George gaped at her blankly. 'After he gave up a world record marlin? Lord save us, Jilly! The man's got to be besotted with you.'

'Oh, no, he's not!' she grated. 'And he's played out his line. The matter's not up for discussion, George. But I'm very, very glad you're going to skipper the boat for the rest of the season. I don't want ever to handle another charter. Not ever again,' she added with vehement feeling.

And lest he try to pursue an argument, Jillian

walked out to the cockpit and propped herself against the stern of the boat, well out of range for a man as incapacitated as old George was this morning. It would be a marvel if he was in a fit state to meet the next charter tomorrow morning. At least the success of this charter guaranteed no argument about the change of skipper, she thought sourly. *Dreamcatcher* was well and truly lead boat now, and no one could say they would be disadvantaged by her father's absence.

The thought of her father still suffering pain from his back brought tears to Jillian's eyes. At least with old George skippering the boat, everything was safe and secure for the future of *Dreamcatcher*, and she would have the time to keep her father company and look after him. Her own dream was dust in her mouth. There never had been and never would be any future in a relationship with Taylor Marshall.

He hailed them from the mother-ship shortly after nine o'clock. Jillian sourly noted that he looked particularly bright and healthy, and not even her embittered gaze could deny that he was still strikingly handsome. Undoubtedly his sleep had been deep and satisfying, untroubled by any unfulfilled dreams. After all he had got everything he wanted.

Bob stirred himself and went to fetch Taylor in the dinghy. Jillian didn't move. With cold and hard determination she mentally rehearsed every word she was going to say to Taylor, and she steeled her heart against any attraction he might still have for her. He smiled at her as he climbed aboard, a warm, intimate smile, and for one nerve-shattering moment, Jillian's resolve wavered. She quickly switched her gaze to Bob, who languidly resumed his sunbathing position, having tied up the dinghy.

Taylor threw a glance around, saw that no one was likely to interrupt their conversation, and raised his eyebrows in puzzled enquiry. 'Why did you leave last night?' he asked quietly. 'I was expecting to have the pleasure of waking up beside you.'

The melting brown eyes singed her defences. Jillian looked out at the empty horizon, angrily reminding herself that he was empty of the emotion which she had given him. She could never trust him again. Never! She poured a calm indifference into her voice. 'I had everything I wanted from you, Taylor. There seemed no point in staying with you after that.'

Dead silence! A silence so long and still that it drew her gaze back to him. All softness had left his expression. His face was as hard as granite, his eyes dark coals that bit into her. For a moment Jillian exulted in the blow to his macho-male pride.

'You don't mean that,' he grated, a strained, harsh sound of anger and pain.

The exultation died. She had succeeded in her purpose but there was no pleasure in it, none at all. Nevertheless, the hard core of bitterness inside her pushed out the well-rehearsed words. 'Don't be chauvinistic, Taylor, please . . . You must know you have a very sexy body, and I wanted to . . .'

His hands grasped her shoulders, fingers digging in hard. 'Don't give me that!' he snapped at her grimly. 'It's nonsense, Jillian, and you know it. You love me. Now, look me in the eye and tell me that.'

She met the fiery challenge in his eyes only briefly before moving her gaze back to the sea, barely retaining her pose of indifference. She was shaken by his touch, even more shaken by the turbulent emotion he was displaying. Was it only wounded pride? It had to be, she told herself sternly.

'Look at me!' he commanded, and shook her when she did not immediately obey. 'You look me in the eye and tell me that, Jillian.'

No! No, she couldn't. She wouldn't give him that satisfaction. Not after what he had said last night. One 'touchdown' was one too many. How dared he demand such an admission from her when not once had he spoken of love. Nor was he declaring any love. Be damned if she would let him draw another surrender from her! Somehow she forced a taunting smile to her lips and veiled her painful vulnerability to him with an arch look of scepticism. 'Are you so arrogant with every woman after you've had sex with her?'

That stopped him. He sucked in a sharp breath and his lips tightened over it. His eyes glittered with disbelief. 'If you only wanted me for . . .' his teeth gritted, '. . . for that purpose, you could have enjoyed it from the first night we met. So what's the truth, Jillian?'

It wasn't fair that he could make her tremble inside. It wasn't fair that she should love someone so much and not be loved in return. It made all of her impulses so fickle and she had to stand firm against what he was doing to her. He didn't care. He couldn't care after what he had done to her. She lifted her chin in proud defiance. 'I wanted it on my terms. Not yours, Taylor.'

'But it was your first time,' he protested sharply, urgently.

Yes, my first and last time with a man who doesn't love me, Jillian thought savagely, but out loud she assumed a careless tone. 'Well, I had to start somewhere.'

He searched her eyes with searing intensity. 'I don't believe you. I can't! It's not true!' he insisted vehemently.

Despite all he had done to her, Jillian weakened. Pride or no pride, she did not want to hurt him. Not any more. A terrible sadness engulfed her.

But Taylor was not finished. His hands gripped even harder and he shook her. 'Tell me...' The words were violently harsh. 'Tell me, syllable by syllable... word by word... that you don't love me.'

Tears filmed her eyes. Why was he tormenting her like this? Hadn't he had his victory? 'It's over!' she choked out at him. 'Please ... don't make it worse than it has to be, Taylor.' She swallowed hard and shook her head in abject misery. 'I'm sorry if I hurt you, truly sorry, but it's better this way. Please don't drag it on.'

'Jillian ...'

He didn't get any further. Old George staggered out to the cockpit, shaking his head miserably from side to side. 'You here, lad? What time is it? Should we be starting?'

Taylor's hands eased away from her. He looked sick as he turned to George. 'The charter is finished.

We're going back to Cairns.' He turned back to Jillian, a hard accusation in his eyes. 'After yesterday, anything else would be an anti-climax.'

'Ah, thank God for that!' old George wheezed.

Jillian met Taylor's hard look with one of tired resignation. His jaw settled into a harsh uncompromising line as she remained silent. 'I'll get Earl and Jerry. We'll be ready to leave as soon as you are,' he said coldly, then turned aside to call Bob to the dinghy.

She watched him go across to the mother-ship with bleak, yearning eyes, still wanting to be one with him with every ounce of her body.

'Are you all right to get the boat ready, lass?' old George croaked shakily.

'Yes, don't worry, George. You'd better go and rest that head of yours,' she answered softly. At least he was her friend. He always would be.

'I'll be all right tomorrow, Jilly,' he assured her. 'I'm going off the grog. Well ... almost. Just the occasional nip at the end of the day to keep me nose sharp.'

She managed a smile. 'And who'd be doubting your word?'

He started to chuckle, then moaned and held his head. 'Tomorrow,' he muttered and staggered back into the cabin.

She set about preparing the boat for the trip back to Cairns and had everything shipshape before the putter of the outboard motor on the dinghy warned her that the Americans were on the way. She quickly retreated to the fly-bridge, not trusting herself to act normally within any close vicinity to Taylor. Bob was obviously mobile enough to look after everyone.

It took some time to lift all the luggage on board. Both Earl and Jerry looked rather green about the gills and were absolutely useless. All in all it seemed that last night had been a disaster for everyone except for Taylor. He handed everything up to Bob who was beginning to recover his usual cheery nature. It appeared that Earl and Jerry were more than content to eschew the day's fishing and get back to terra firma. Taylor helped Bob stow the dinghy on board and gave her a curt wave to get going.

No one came up to the fly-bridge, and Jillian had it all to herself for the whole trip to Cairns. She stood alone, as she always would be from now on, she thought despairingly. She couldn't imagine ever loving another man after Taylor. As old George had sadly said of himself, she just hadn't been good enough. Taylor was the one that got away, not her. She had been caught, tagged, and released, just like the giant marlin, except the tag was in her heart and she could not believe she would ever be caught again.

They said goodbye at the jetty. Earl and Jerry had recovered their spirits somewhat, and their friendly farewells were in sharp contrast to their greetings on that fateful first day of fishing. But Taylor's leave-taking was cool and clipped. He was stern-faced, very dignified and terribly, terribly remote. Jillian watched them go. No one threw even one backward glance at her.

The charter was over, as she had always known it would be over, just another holiday experience for the

Americans that would be talked about amongst their friends for a while. Taylor Marshall would soon be surrounded by girls of his own kind back in the States and he would quickly forget her. No doubt he would find her eminently forgettable.

Never in her life had she felt so bereft, so lonely and destitute. So sick at heart that she could barely function, Jillian drove herself to organise a division of the chores that had to be done for the next charter. Bob and old George were to see to the boat, the baits, and the restocking of the bar. She made herself responsible for getting in the food stores. Then, holding grimly to the last shreds of control, she left the boat and drove home to Holloways Beach where she crumpled up and cried tears of utter desolation.

By mid-afternoon she had pulled herself together enough to shower and change into fresh clothes. The mauve and white dress she chose was an attractive style, its circular skirt graceful and its loosely gathered bodice finished in shoestring straps over her shoulders. Jillian slipped on white sandals, carefully hid all signs of distress with make-up, then, satisfied that her father would see nothing amiss with her appearance, she drove in to the hospital.

Jack Howard was still in a lot of discomfort but he looked much more himself. His face was less grey and strained, and all anxiety had cleared from his eyes. They twinkled happily at Jillian. 'And how's the world record skipper today?' he teased with a deep note of pride in his voice.

She forced a smile. 'I see the grapevine has been busy again.

He grinned. 'I hear that all Cairns is buzzing with the story, and Earl Schultz dropped in earlier to give me chapter and verse. You did a great job, Jilly. Better than I could do myself.'

Earl Schultz, not Taylor Marshall, Jillian thought despondently. It was plain that Taylor was well and truly finished with the Howards. 'I wouldn't say that, Dad,' she sighed, then offered another smile. 'Anyhow, old George has agreed to skipper for the rest of the season, so tomorrow I can take you home and look after you. Isn't that great?'

Her father beamed at her. 'Well, I can't say I won't be glad to get out of this hospital bed. But what about you, Jilly? I would've thought your success would make you eager . . .'

'It was really old George's success, Dad,' she cut in quickly. 'He told me where to go all the time. To tell you the truth I'll be relieved to get back to the boutique. Skippering is a a hard responsibility to carry. I don't know how you can enjoy it.'

His eyes crinkled happily at her. 'I guess it's in the blood, Jilly. It's all I've ever wanted to do, and thanks to you, I'll be able to carry on.'

Yes, at least she had accomplished that, Jillian consoled herself bleakly. 'How's Gordon, Dad? Have you seen him lately?'

'Yes, we were talking this morning. His hand is mending fine and he's going back to the States with the others tomorrow, but he'll be back next year.' Her father gave her a conspiratorial grin. 'I've offered to take him on as second deckie for the season, turn him into a real professional.'

'That was nice of you, Dad.'

'Ah, he's got fishing in his blood, too. He'll be good.'

Unfortunately he would remind Jillian of Taylor, but that was a petty thought, she chided herself. 'Well I've got to pick up the provisions for the next charter, Dad,' she said quickly, fighting back another rush of tears at the thought of Taylor. She stood up and kissed her father. 'I'll see you in the morning. OK?'

He squeezed her hand feelingly. 'Fine, Jilly. Just fine. And you have a good rest tonight. You look a bit pale and drawn. Guess it has been a strain for you, being skipper.'

'Well, it's all over now,' she murmured and dropped another kiss on his forehead before leaving.

All over. The words were a dull throb in her mind as she did the rounds of the stores, picking up the necessary provisions. She thought fleetingly of dropping in on Pamela, but was in no mood for chatting. Pamela and the boutique could wait until tomorrow. Or the next day. When she felt up to resuming the shattered pieces of her old life. She would put it all back together somehow, but it would never be the same. She knew that with all the certainty of the pain in her heart.

Old George was still on board when she returned to the boat, waiting to help her stack the provisions into the main freezer. He had sobered up considerably and swore he wouldn't touch another drop of whisky for weeks. The boat was spick and span. Terry Lewis, her father's second deckie, had called by, checking back in for the next charter. Bob had gone home. There was nothing else to do except see the next charter at the hotel and explain the change of skipper, but Jillian was sure there would be no problems over that now.

Old George clapped her on the shoulder. 'Well, I suppose you'll be wanting to go and be with the lad,' he said indulgently. 'I'll leave the boat in proper order for you, Jilly.'

She could not stop the hurt from creeping into her voice. 'I told you that was over, George.'

'Over?' He sounded incredulous.

It was plain he didn't remember their conversation this morning or the sight of her and Taylor together in the cockpit had given him a different impression. Jillian shrugged. 'It was only a holiday . . . affair.' She almost choked over the word.

'Are you crazy, lass? Don't tell me you're not in love with the man. It was written all over you when he let that world-record go.'

She flashed him a pained look. 'Forget it, George. He will, soon enough,' she added bitterly.

Old George shook his head. 'Didn't look that way to me. Looked to me as if he couldn't think of anything but you. Didn't want to be with his mates. Didn't even want his fish. He had it real bad for you, Jilly, and to my old eyes, that only comes with loving a woman. I reckon you've read him wrong. Now whatever you've said to each other, you go and fix it up. Don't let him get away, Jilly. You'll regret it the rest of your life. Speaking as one who knows,' he added sadly.

Could he be right about Taylor? A sliver of hope writhed through her despair. Was it possible that she had misunderstood Taylor last night, that she had taken the wrong meaning from his words? She recalled his puzzlement this morning, his vehemence and his hurt. Maybe she had made a terrible mistake.

Old George squeezed her shoulder. 'Go and see him, lass. Get it straightened out,' he advised gently, seeing the agony of uncertainty in her eyes.

But it was not so simple. Not after that awful scene this morning. Jillian stewed over the situation for hours, swinging between the belief that Taylor had surely played her for a fool, and the remote possibility that he had been sincere in his actions, even though his words had been far too open to misinterpretation.

She had to visit the Pacific International Hotel to speak to the new charter anyway. She finally made up her mind to see Taylor and speak to him. Her pain couldn't get any worse even if she made a fool of herself over him. George was right. It was better to know than to always wonder if she had been wrong.

The new charter was a very charming Englishman who readily accepted the change of skipper, once she had outlined old George's credentials. He held her up, eager to chat over the season's fishing so far and expressing the hope that the marlin would run well for him. Jillian was finally able to extract herself and her heart was thumping wildly as she took the lift up to the eleventh floor.

It was nine-thirty. She hoped Taylor was in his room. She hoped he was alone. She hoped he hadn't gone to bed. She hoped he really did love her. And all these hopes twisted into an agony of longing as she screwed her courage to the sticking point and knocked on his door.

It seemed an eternity before it was opened. Taylor stared blankly at her for a moment, then he leaned back against the opened door, his eyes hard with cynicism, a curl of amusement on his lips, as he waved an invitation to enter. 'How nice of you to call,' he drawled. 'Come and join the party. Earl and Jerry were just saying what good entertainment value you were, Jillian.'

She flinched at the sardonic emphasis he gave to 'entertainment value'. She hadn't been wrong. That was how he had thought of her. She took a step back and swallowed to moisten a throat that had gone impossibly dry. She was dying inside but she had to hang on a few moments longer. It was the last time she would ever see him. 'I ... I only came to say goodbye.'

'Oh, I'm sure we can do more than that for you.' His eyes glittered with contempt. 'We could give you another sexual experience. Why not try a good old gang-bang? There are endless possibilities.'

Tears of humiliation stung her eyes. She opened her mouth to deny his cruel words but no sound came out. She turned away and, forcing her trembling legs to move, she walked down a corridor which was suddenly swaying and tilting.

'Jillian!'

The sharp cry penetrated the terrible fog in her mind. Even now he could still get to her, making her turn towards his call. She looked back at him through a film of tears.

'I'm sorry,' he said curtly. 'That was uncalled for.'

'It doesn't matter,' she croaked out. Nothing mattered any more.

His hands moved in a gesture of disgust. 'I didn't mean it,' he said regretfully.

'It doesn't matter,' she repeated dully, and a thread of pride made her add, 'I just wanted to thank you again for taking the charter. It . . . it meant a lot to my father . . . and me. I wish you well, Taylor.'

'Jillian . . .'

'No, please . . . don't say any more.' She couldn't bear it. Couldn't bear even seeing him. She turned blindly, hurried her steps to the lift and almost fell against the 'down' button.

'Goodbye . . . honey-girl.'

The words floated after her, a soft waft of sound that Jillian wasn't even sure she really heard. But they held the echo of finality that was impossible now not to acknowledge. It was over.

CHAPTER TEN

JILLIAN threw herself into a frenzy of house-cleaning, determined to have everything tidy and cheerful for her father when she brought him home from hospital, and equally determined to stop agonising over her love for Taylor Marshall. She had spent a seemingly endless night of utter misery, but she would survive, Jillian decided stubbornly. She could and would live without him. But when she unpacked the suitcase of clothes she had taken on the boat, and saw the wattle-dress hanging in her wardrobe, she snatched it out, marched straight to the incinerator in the back yard, and burnt it. And the words from the burial service echoed mournfully through her mind ... ashes to ashes.

An aeroplane droned overheard. She hurried back into the house, not looking up to see if it was coming into Cairns or leaving. She would never be able to hear an aeroplane again without its reminding her of Taylor. She knew he would be flying out today, but it might as well have been last night. It did not matter. He was gone from her life and he was never coming back.

Jillian kept herself extremely busy the next few days, looking after her father, cooking all his favourite foods, weeding the garden, even cleaning all the house windows. Jack Howard naturally wanted to know all the details about the charter and Jillian gradually got quite adept at blocking any personal thought of Taylor out of her mind when she spoke of him. He became 'the angler' not the man.

At the beginning of the next week she went back to the boutique, and, having had a great deal of practice with her father, she was able to answer all of Pamela's questions with a convincing show of equanimity. The weeks rolled on. The boutique did a brisk tourist trade, and Jillian kept on the girl whom Pamela had hired. Not only was she a good saleswoman, but she gave Jillian the time off to spend a long lunchtime with her father every day.

It was just prior to one such lunchtime that Pamela called Jillian aside in a conspiratorial manner. 'I've met a fabulous guy, Jillian, and I desperately want him to notice me. I mean really notice me. He's going to be at a party I'm invited to on Saturday night and I thought...' She drew in a deep breath. 'Well, I thought if I could borrow that wattle-dress from you...'

'No!' Jillian answered sharply.

Too sharply. Pamela looked affronted. 'I didn't think you'd mind.'

Jillian bit her lips and turned aside as pain stabbed into her heart 'It's not that I mind, but that's not the way to attract a man, Pamela. Take my word for it,' she added bitterly.

'But you got away with it,' Pamela expostulated. 'And you got what you wanted, didn't you?'

Jillian turned bleak, pain-washed eyes on her friend. 'No, I didn't get away with it. And no, I didn't get what I wanted. I lost . . . everything.' She drew in a shuddering breath in an attempt to counteract the pain and offered a wry smile. 'Don't ask me about it, Pamela. I don't ever want to talk about it. And anyway, I burnt the dress.'

Pamela looked like a stunned mullet but, like the good friend she was, she didn't talk about it and never tried to.

Life went on. The fishing season ended with *Dreamcatcher* the lead boat by a record margin. Jack Howard's back was slowly mending. Old George spent a leisurely weekend with the Howards, recounting his successes with all the relish of a man reborn to fishing.

'Twice I hooked up a world record, Jack, but the anglers didn't have the stamina or the strength to haul them in. Not like Taylor Marshall, eh Jilly?'

'No,' she murmured, wishing fiercely that old George had not brought up the name. She had been trying very hard to keep Taylor Marshall out of her thoughts. He would certainly not be thinking of her, she told herself miserably.

Old George frowned, suddenly conscious of his *faux pas*. Only once had he questioned her about what had happened with Taylor since that last day of the charter and Jillian had told him she didn't want to hear Taylor's name mentioned again.

'Been thinking of going to Hawaii,' he said brightly. 'I've never had a go at the blue marlin. Heard tell it's a better fighting fish than the black, but I'll have to see that to believe it.' Then he added even more brightly, 'How about you coming with me,

Jilly? Have a good holiday. I'll pay for the trip. Thanks to Jack here, I'm flush with money and no one to spend it on.'

She shook her head. 'I don't really fancy going fishing, George.'

'Leave the fishing to me. You can relax on the beaches, meet other people, have a good time. I reckon you could do with a break away from here and your dad will surely be back in trim soon. No worries.'

She knew he meant it kindly and thanked him for the offer, but she wasn't interested in going anywhere. The truth was, she had lost interest in everything, even life itself. But her father was also concerned about her and the two men eventually pestered her into saying she would think about it.

But that wasn't good enough for old George. He insisted on presuming she would definitely come with him and hounded her for weeks about getting a passport. For the sake of peace she went through the necessary officialdom. Eventually her father was fit enough to go back to work and she missed his company on the days he had charters for light-tackle or bottom-line fishing. Her life seemed increasingly empty.

Week followed week. Time became meaningless. Old George kept bringing up Hawaii, dropping brochures in to her, urging her to make choices about hotels or tours. Pamela tried to include Jillian in her social life with invitations to parties, but after accepting one invitation to appease her friend's concern, she resolutely refused all others. She couldn't even pretend superficial gaiety and the sight of other people apparently in happy relationships only increased her feeling of desolation.

Month followed month. Then one day Jillian was busy with a customer in a fitting-room when Pamela virtually pounced on her, her eyes alight with excitement. 'There's a man out the front asking to see you. An American! He said he had a charter with you last season.,

Taylor? Taylor come back to see her? Jillian's heart stopped, then beat so hard she felt dizzy. She forgot the customer. Pamela was only a dim figure. She could see Taylor Marshall in her mind, as clearly as if he was before her now, and she walked out into the main salon of the shop, her whole body tingling with blissful hope.

Earl Schultz came forward to greet her. The blood drained from Jillian's face. Her disppointment was so savage she had to grip on to a rack of dresses to hold herself steady. It wasn't Taylor. Of course it wouldn't be Taylor, she told herself with a lashing of self-contempt for being so stupid as to think it might be. But what was Earl Schultz doing here?

He frowned at her. 'Are you OK?'

'Yes. Yes, of course. How nice to see you again,' she forced out with a stiffly polite smile.

'You don't look so good,' he observed tactlessly.

'I'm fine,' Jillian lied. 'And you? What can I do for you?'

'I want to talk to you. This is your boutique, isn't it? You can leave it and come and have lunch with me?' he demanded more than asked.

She frowned. It was only eleven-thirty, early for

lunch, but there was no reason why she couldn't go. But what was Earl Schultz doing here, and why did he want to talk to her? 'My father's well now Earl. In fact he's at home today. If you . . .'

'I haven't flown half-way around the damned world to talk about fishing,' he retorted irritably, then made a visible effort to recover his poise and offer an appeasing smile. 'I'm sorry for being curt with you, but I've come on a matter of considerable importance, and I'd be very much obliged if you'll come back to the hotel with me and hear me out.'

Jillian was totally bewildered. She couldn't imagine what matter of importance could have brought Earl Schultz to her, but clearly he did not intend to be put off. She signalled Pamela that she was going, all too aware of the irony of her friend's curious ogling, then turned to the American with a slight nod. 'I can spare you an hour.'

'Let's go then,' he said impatiently, and Jillian was reminded of the chauvinistic arrogance he had shown when they had first met.

She went with him but his brusque manner aroused a ready antagonism. He was pushing her around, and she didn't like the feeling. It reminded her of how Taylor had manipulated her last season and that brought back the pain. Earl steered her into the Marketplace all-day snack-bar in the Pacific International and sat her down at a table, taking the seat opposite her. His rather sharp face looked harried and tense. He accepted the menus from the waitress with barely concealed irritation, and ordered Barramundi for both of them without even consulting

Jillian. Then he sat back and eyed her with a brooding air.

'May I ask what brought you back to Cairns?' Jillian asked rather impatiently.

'Would I be mistaken in thinking you were disappointed that I wasn't Taylor?' he retorted bluntly.

Jillian didn't answer. After the initial shock of his attack she was busy erecting some protective defences.

Earl leaned forward, his eyes sharp with probing urgency. 'I don't think you can deny that you and Taylor got pretty close while we were here. What I want to know is how close?'

'I don't think that's any of your business,' Jillian replied tightly.

'Do you still feel anything for him?'

She didn't answer, glaring her resentment at such a personal intrusion.

Earl Schultz pulled a grimace of frustration. 'All right, we'll take another tack. As I understand it, that charter was damned important to you and your father last season. If Taylor hadn't decided to take it up, your father would have lost his boat. Is that correct?'

'If the other charters had cancelled too,' she corrected him coldly.

'But Taylor gave you your best chance, didn't he?' Earl persisted.

'Yes,' she admitted reluctantly.

'Then it seems to me that you owe him.'

Jillian clenched her teeth. 'Would you mind getting

to the point? What has Taylor Marshall to do with all this?'

Earl sighed and shook his head. 'At the present moment he's wrecking his whole damned career and if he doesn't pull his act together very smartly he'll be out of pro football. And that's his life, Jillian, like the boat is your father's life. Make no mistake about that. Without Taylor your father might have lost his boat. I figure you owe him two weeks of your time.'

Jillian was totally confused by the argument. 'What do you mean? I don't understand what you're saying.'

'I want you to come back to the States with me.'

A wild flash of hope burst through her mind. 'Did Taylor ask you to . . .'

'Hell, no!'

The hope died. 'Then would you please explain what you want of me?' she asked flatly.

He sighed in exasperation. 'To tell you the truth I don't know myself, but I care about that boy and I'll try anything that might help.' He flicked her an anxious look of appeal. 'I don't know what happened between you two. All I know is he hasn't been the same since. Can't seem to find the kind of motivation he used to have. Not interested in girls. Not interested in any damned thing. I thought once he got back to playing football . . . Goddammit, he was the star quarterback, and now he's nothing more than a hack!'

He slammed his fist down on the table in exasperation. 'Something's got to be done and you're the only answer I've got left. I'll pay for the trip. I'll pay all your expenses for two weeks in the States. Maybe you can perform some miracle on him. I don't know. But as far as I'm concerned it's worth a chance. And that's why I'm here.'

Jillian's head was whirling. Taylor hadn't been interested in any girl since her. From Earl's description he was finding life as empty as she did without him. Maybe he really did love her. He had virtually begged her that last morning to admit her love for him. Pride had stopped her and it could be that pride had stopped him from confessing his love for her. And between her pride and his they had reached a point of no return. There was no decision to be made. Jillian desperately wanted to see Taylor again, even if the visit should prove futile.

'I'll come with you.'

Earl started out of his momentary abstraction. 'You will?'

She nodded.

He heaved a sigh of relief. Then his eyes narrowed on her 'May I ask why? Don't get me wrong, but I didn't expect this mission to be so easy.'

She gave him a dry smile. 'I'd like to see Taylor playing football.'

He pulled a wry grimace. 'I hope to God you do! The kind of football he should be playing! I don't know how this is going to work out, Jillian,' he added anxiously. 'I'm only playing a hunch.'

'That's OK. I get a free holiday, don't I? Like you got a free day's fishing,' she reminded him with a touch of irony.

He flashed her a reluctant look of admiration.

'You're quite a girl! Taylor might do a lot worse than you if that's the way the wind blows. And before you take umbrage, that's a compliment. Now let's work out a travel plan.'

It seemed doubly ironic to Jillian that the passport she had obtained for a holiday designed to get her mind off Taylor should be used to get back to him, but she was intensely grateful now for old George's pushing. The only real difficulty about the trip was breaking the news to her father.

'But Jilly, what has all this got to do with you? Why should you go haring off to America?' he demanded in bewilderment.

Finally she gave her father the truth. 'Because if Taylor Marshall needs me in any way, I have to go to him, Dad. I love him. I don't think I'll ever stop loving him.'

Her answer stunned him for a few moments, then slowly he nodded his head. 'So that's what it's all been about these last few months.' He sighed and lifted sadly appealing eyes to her. 'Am I losing a daughter, Jilly?'

'You'll never lose me, Dad,' she assured him. 'Whatever happens, I'll always be your daughter.'

They hugged one another, sharing a closer understanding than they had ever shared before.

Earl Schultz wasted no time. He was anxious to get back for Taylor's next football game which was in Miami, Florida, and the finalised travelling schedule was a gruelling one. The long trip was passed in a strange, emotional limbo for Jillian. She did not really know what she was flying towards, and she hardly dared to hope that there might be any lasting happiness for her at the end of the journey. But there was one very firm resolution in her mind. This time when she saw Taylor, she would be completely honest with him. No pride. No prevarication. No shrinking inside herself.

They changed aeroplanes several times. The airports in America seemed huge and bewildering to Jillian, and people talked in such different accents it was sometimes difficult to understand their speech. Earl kept bustling her along. More and more she felt a fish out of water. They were two hours late arriving at their destination, and Earl was in a high state of tension.

'No time for going to a hotel. We've got to get to the stadium,' he muttered, rushing her through the terminal.

Jillian did not mind. Physically she was so tired she was just about floating, but the anticipation of seeing Taylor again filled her with a nervous excitement that kept exhaustion at bay.

The game had already started when the taxi dropped them at the stadium. Earl Schultz flicked some special pass to a number of officials who tried to bar their way. There was considerable argument over admitting Jillian, but Earl somehow talked her through and they were eventually admitted to an area where there were a lot of players sitting on benches or milling around at the side of the football field.

Jillian had thought Taylor a big man, but these men in their padded football uniforms looked like veritable giants. She remembered that Taylor had told her that his team was called the Giants, which seemed very fitting, and Earl had said they were playing the Broncos today. There seemed to be too many players on and off the field until Jillian recalled reading that each team really had three teams, one for offence, one for defence, and specialist players who did kick-offs and punts and whatever.

Jillian's eyes darted backwards and forwards but she couldn't spot Taylor anywhere, and she began to doubt she would recognise him since the men on the field and even some on the sidelines wore helmets with a kind of grille over their faces. She decided this sport must be terribly dangerous if they had to wear so much protective gear. 'Do you know where Taylor is?' she whispered to Earl Schultz.

He pointed. 'The man standing at the back on the playing field.'

Suddenly the two lines of men on the field moved and the ball was thrown back to Taylor. Jillian watched in mesmerised horror as he backpedalled, seemed to stumble, and two huge men shaped like gorillas hammered into him. He fell like a sack of potatoes. He had to be hurt. He had to be terribly hurt. Without stopping to think, Jillian started running towards him. Restraining hands grasped her shoulders. She tried to struggle free.

A bull of a man, obviously some maniac, was jumping up and down and screaming above the roar of the crowd. 'Get rid of that crazy dame! Take her away!'

Jillian kept fighting the man who was dragging her backwards. 'For Chrissake!' Earl was yelling. 'It's a

two thousand dollar fine if you cross that line!'
Everyone was yelling. The whole stadium seemed to
be in an uproar. But Jillian was only concerned about
Taylor. To her huge relief she saw that he was
climbing to his feet. He wasn't injured.

Someone was shouting 'Time-out!' and Taylor
looked towards the maniac but his gaze didn't quite
reach him. It stopped on her. She began struggling
against the restraining hands again as Taylor ran
towards her. He was taking off his helmet and she
could see his face properly and he looked wonderful,
even though his body was all distorted with padding.

'Jillian! Jillian!' he called incredulously.

The hands finally released her and she staggered a
few steps into the safe secure arms of Taylor
Marshall. No matter that she was a fish out of water so
long as he caught her. 'What are you doing here?' he
asked, harsh emotion in his voice.

Jillian was too befuddled to think of a sensible
reply. Her eyes were swimming in the wonderful dark
depths of his. 'Earl said you needed me and I love you,
Taylor. I love you,' she spilled out helplessly.

His arms almost squeezed the life out of her and to
Jillian's vast relief, Taylor's mouth descended on
hers, sweetly devouring her own starved lips.

'What the hell do you think you're doing!' The
maniac's scream was close and intrusive. Hands were
trying to tear them apart. Taylor reluctantly lifted his
head and looked at the madman, who was just about
frothing at the mouth. He was not the only one upset.
The whole stadium seemed to be booing and various
missiles were being hurled by the crowd.

'If you don't get your act together, Marshall, you're out, and you can spend your whole life with this crazy woman. Who let her in here anyhow?' the maniac raved.

Taylor set Jillian down, grinned at her and then at the maniac. 'Just leave her here and I'll play all right. Shotgun.'

'Hell no!' the maniac grated. 'Then they'll be sure it's a pass play. They'll kill you!'

Taylor laughed, slipped his helmet back on, and ran back on to the field.

Jillian turned anxiously to Earl. 'They won't kill him, will they?'

The maniac threw her a malevolent look. 'If he doesn't come good with something, I will.'

Jillian decided she had better keep her mouth shut. The uproar from the crowd subsided as Taylor's team went into a huddle, but when they lined out and Taylor dropped back several yards, the fans rumbled disapproval again. Someone on the Broncos team yelled 'Pass!' and the whole line moved up closer to the Giants. The maniac groaned as Taylor called the signals.

Then suddenly the ball flew back to Taylor. He turned quickly towards the right flank but he didn't pass the ball. Two huge Bronco defenders charged across the line, bumped off the obvious receiver and headed for Taylor. Jillian tensed. A big Giant blocked one of them and another Giant ran past Taylor, heading for a vacant hole that had opened up as the Bronco line had moved to the left. Taylor tucked the ball away and followed hard on his heels.

The two of them broke through the Bronco line. The Giant in front of Taylor smothered a Bronco defender. Taylor skirted their tumbling bodies and accelerated, weaving his way downfield with knees pumping high. As he crossed the midfield stripe, the one remaining Bronco defender made a desperate dive. It almost seemed that Taylor floated around him, leaving him flat on his face. From that second on it was a foot-race to the goal-line and the Broncos had no chance.

Jillian watched him run, tall and lean and powerful and beautiful, a great champion in full flight. A surge of adrenalin pumped through her tired body as she exulted in the sheer glory of the man she loved. The roar of the crowd as Taylor reached the end-zone was a sound Jillian would never forget. Taylor placed the ball on the ground, a backfield judge put both hands parallel over his head, and it seemed to Jillian that the whole stadium rose up in wild jubilation.

'Touchdown!'

The word rang in her ears again and again, sending shivers down her spine. This moment of wild exultation was a touchdown? She looked apprehensively at Taylor. He had started running back, evading his team-mates who were trying to thump him on the back. He was running in a direct line to her and he swept Jillian off her feet and swung her in a high circle as one would a child. She thumped back against him and he wrapped his arms around her, his face alight with jubilant happiness.

Before either of them could say a word, the maniac was throwing his arms around them both. 'How did you do it? Goddamn! How did you do it?' he was screaming now.

Taylor grinned at Jillian then grinned at the maniac. 'Coach, this is the lady who taught me how to bait a hook . . .' His gaze dropped back to Jillian, and the brown eyes were more melting than she had ever seen them. '. . . and I love her. I love her more than anything else in the world.'

'That had better not mean football,' the coach threatened. 'And no more running. You want your legs broken? You're supposed to pass the damned ball!' But his fierce look held a gleam of indulgence and he left them alone until Taylor had to go back on to the field to play.

The rest of the game passed in a gloriously happy daze for Jillian. Two more touchdowns were scored. Everyone said that Taylor was playing brilliantly and she stood there between Earl and the maniac-coach, almost bursting with pride for the man she loved. And he loved her. He really did love her. He had thanked Earl profusely for bringing her to him and his eyes had been brimming with emotion.

The game was well and truly won and afterwards Taylor took her to his hotel. In the privacy of his room, they held each other for a long time, not speaking, not even kissing, just savouring the magic of being together.

'Do you know how many times I've dreamed of this?' Taylor murmured huskily, his mouth grazing softly across her hair. 'I thought I had to be dreaming when I looked up and saw you today. Why wouldn't you admit you loved me when I asked, Jillian? What did I do wrong? When we made love I felt so complete, so on top of the world, and then the next morning, you made me feel like . . . like nothing.'

The memory of too much pain was in his voice and Jillian reached up to kiss him, hoping to wipe it away. 'You never said you loved me Taylor. I thought you really cared for me when we made love, but afterwards you talked of your pride, and your determination to catch me, and scoring a touchdown. I thought I'd only been a challenge to you and you'd got all you wanted from me.'

He shuddered in recoil from her words. 'No. Never. For me it was the beginning, not an end, Jillian.' He drew back slightly and gently cupped her face, his eyes projecting an intense sincerity. 'Please believe that. And as for my damned pride, I've learnt a great deal about humility since then. To think if only I'd laid myself open to you . . .' He closed his eyes and swallowed hard. 'And but for Earl I would still be without you.'

'It was my fault, too, Taylor. It scared me how much you affected me. Most of the time I was trying to protect myself. There just wasn't enough time to . . . to believe you loved me,' she explained ruefully.

'Oh, honey-girl!' he sighed, and opened softly adoring eyes. 'I think I fell in love with you that first afternoon when you were challenging me about catching a world record fish, but I didn't know it for sure until I actually caught that giant marlin. I knew then that you meant more to me than any world record. I thought you understood. As for saying "touchdown", that didn't relate back to what I'd said before, Jillian. To a football player, it means the ultimate goal, and that's what I felt I'd reached with you that night. Do you understand?'

'Now I do. But then I felt so hurt . . .' She searched his eyes anxiously. 'I was hitting back at you the next morning, Taylor. I didn't mean any of the things I said. I wanted to tell you the truth when I came up to your room that last night, but . . .'

'But I didn't let you,' he finished with heavy regret. 'We've wasted a lot of time, honey-girl. Do you love me enough to marry me and share my life?'

'Yes,' she answered with heartfelt fervour.

His smile was full of triumphant delight. 'Then I really have caught you this time and you're never getting away again.'

Her smile was one of utter contentment. 'I don't want to get away.'

'In that case, if I make love to you and happen to fall asleep afterwards, you'll still be there beside me when I wake up.'

'I think it might be me who falls asleep this time. I'm dead-beat, Taylor,' she teased lightly.

He laughed and swept her up in his arms to carry her over to his bed where he laid her down very lovingly. 'I seem to recall saying something like that, but it didn't stop you seducing me. I have a fancy to return the favour.'

'Mmm . . . I think I might fancy that,' she murmured, pulling him down with her.

But they were so hungry for each other that any thought of seduction was soon forgotten, as was everything else until they lay together in complete satiation.

'We can spend some time in Cairns every year, can't we, Taylor?' Jillian asked drowsily. 'Dad will miss me."

'Sure we will. Have to catch up on some more of old George's stories.'

'And Taylor, please try not to get sacked in your next football game. I didn't like seeing those horrible big men piling on top of you.'

He laughed until tears ran down his cheeks. 'Oh, honey-girl! Was that why you were trying to run on to the field?'

'I thought you were hurt.'

He suddenly sobered and kissed her with almost reverent tenderness. 'I was, but not physically. I've been hurting for months. Right up until I saw you today. I love you so much, Jillian. Don't ever leave me.

'You're my life,' she whispered. 'I'll always love you and be with you wherever you go.'

Taylor smiled his deep pleasure in her, then broke into laughter again. 'Well, the coach might have something to say about that, but from me you'll get no argument, honey-girl. For ever and amen.'

Jillian snuggled closer to him, basking in the safe, protective custody of Taylor's arms. It was where she wanted to be, where she had dreamed so often of being. Now she was there. For ever. As she slowly drifted into sleep she murmured, 'I love you.'

And hearing her, Taylor whispered back, 'I'll never leave you, ever again.' His arms tightened around her, and he gently drew Jillian down to the warmth and comfort that only he could give her. And she slept with a smile of utter peace on her lips.

Harlequin Presents

Coming Next Month

Available in January wherever paperback books are sold, or through
Harlequin Reader Service:

In the U.S.
901 Fuhrmann Blvd.
P.O. Box 1397
Buffalo, N.Y. 14240-1397

In Canada
P.O. Box 603
Fort Erie, Ontario
L2A 5X3

**For the millions who can't read
Give the Gift of Literacy**

One out of five adults in North America
cannot read or write well enough
to fill out a job application
or understand the directions on a bottle of medicine.

**You can change all this by joining the fight
against illiteracy.**

For more information write to:
Contact, Box 81826, Lincoln, Neb. 68501
In the United States, call toll free: 1-800-228-8813

**The only degree you need
is a degree of caring**

"This ad made possible with the cooperation of the Coalition for Literacy and the Ad Council."
Give the Gift of Literacy Campaign is a project of the book and periodical industry,
in partnership with Telephone Pioneers of America.

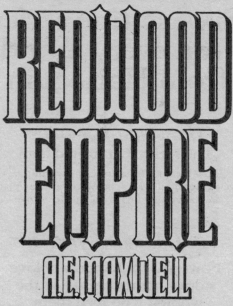

Six exciting series for you every month... from Harlequin

Harlequin Romance·
The series that started it all

Tender, captivating and heartwarming...
love stories that sweep you off to faraway places
and delight you with the magic of love.

◆

Harlequin Presents·
Powerful contemporary love stories...as individual as the women who read them

The No. 1 romance series...
exciting love stories for you, the woman of today...
a rare blend of passion and dramatic realism.

◆

Harlequin Superromance®
It's more than romance...
it's Harlequin Superromance

A sophisticated, contemporary romance-fiction
series, providing you with a longer,
more involving read...a richer mix of complex plots,
realism and adventure.

Harlequin American Romance™
Harlequin celebrates the American woman...

...by offering you romance stories written about American women, by American women for American women. This series offers you contemporary romances uniquely North American in flavor and appeal.

◆

Harlequin Temptation™
Passionate stories for today's woman

An exciting series of sensual, mature stories of love...dilemmas, choices, resolutions... all contemporary issues dealt with in a true-to-life fashion by some of your favorite authors.

◆

Harlequin Intrigue
Because romance can be quite an adventure

Harlequin Intrigue, an innovative series that blends the romance you expect... with the unexpected. Each story has an added element of intrigue that provides a new twist to the Harlequin tradition of romance excellence.

Harlequin Books®

PROD-A-2

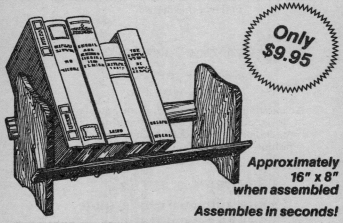